THE TROUBLE WITH TRYING TO DATE A MURDERER

MURDER SPREES AND MUTE DECREES, BOOK ONE

JENNIFER CODY

The Trouble with Trying to Date a Murderer, Copyright 2022 Jennifer Cody
Amazon Edition

All rights reserved. This book or any portion thereof may not be reproduced or used in any manner whatsoever without the express written permission of the publisher except for the use of brief quotations in a book review.

This book is a work of fiction. Names, characters, places, organizations and incidents are either products of the author's imagination or used fictitiously. Any resemblance to actual persons, living or dead, events or organizations is entirely coincidental.

Formatting and Cover Design by Tammy Basile, Aspen Tree E.A.S.

Editing by Shannon, Aspen Tree E.A.S.

AMAZON EDITION, LICENSE NOTES

This e-book is licensed for your personal enjoyment only. This e-book may not be re-sold or given away to other people. If you would like to share this book with another person, please purchase an additional copy for each recipient. If you are reading this book and did not purchase it, or it was not purchased for your use only, then please return to your favorite e-book retailer and purchase your own copy. Thank you for respecting the hard work of this author.

THANK YOU NOTE

Thank you to my incomparable betas, Carol, Cameron, Tessa, Nichole, and Janine. Thank you to Shannon for proofreading! Thank you to Tammy for all your work, love, support, and encouragement; you are an amazing PA and friend. Thank you to my Beardo for listening to me going on about how much I loved this book, for always supporting me no matter my endeavors, and for loving my dark, little, evil heart.

A NOTE FROM ROMILY

Dear Reader,
    I'm a sassy, brave, beautiful boy who happens to use humor to cope with an unseen disability. If that bothers you, maybe you should consider expanding your horizons about how disabled people make life bearable when we're surrounded by the oblivious.

Sincerely,
    Romily Butcher

PS: There's a dub-con scene in this book. Shhh, it's ok. I'm fine.

CHAPTER ONE

Once upon a time, a mute boy fell in love with an unapologetic murderer.

Ok, it happened last Thursday at the diner where I'd worked for all of thirty minutes before a man wearing shit kickers, a black A-shirt, yoga pants, and like a hundred pounds of guns and ammo came into the diner and called out, "Steak and eggs, scrambled with sourdough, and a black coffee."

The man didn't even sit, he just announced his order.

And then all hell broke loose.

Every patron in the diner started attacking him with bullets and knives and their bodies. All the man wanted was some breakfast and suddenly all the other customers wanted him dead. I watched in absolute horror with my back pressed up against the wall as the man shredded every person in the diner. It wasn't even a one-at-a-time thing. I saw him get a two-fer with one of his hand guns, and when one of my customers tried to get him with a sword—like, where did he even get a fucking sword?—the man stole the sword and skewered two people onto one of the metal tables. *With the goddamn sword.* By the time the stragglers were starting to realize that thirty against one was maybe a bit unfair odds in his favor, the diner was probably never going to reopen, and I wasn't holding out much hope of getting paid for my hour.

As the last person dropped with a death gurgle, the cook rang the bell. "Order up!"

The man, breathing hard and covered in the crimson flow of life and death—i.e., blood—looked at me, straightened his back, and adjusted his armory. "Can I get that to go?"

And that's how I ended up boxing up a murderer's breakfast and possibly falling in love, because even though he wasn't particularly handsome or incredibly charming, he was competent and self-possessed, and if no one ever told you that confidence is sexy, then allow me to be the first: confidence is sexy. Full stop. I don't care what you look like or if you have a bad personality or if you're homely. Confidence. Is. Sexy.

And really, it's not like I hadn't been through two other mass murders in my life. This wasn't my first rodeo, and I'm a firm believer in third time's the charm, so of course when I handed the man a bag with his breakfast in it and our hands brushed, I got flutters and butterflies and a heaping spoon of regret that I would probably never meet the man again.

He handed me a hundred-dollar bill and left. Le sigh. My one true love, whatever his name was…

At least I got paid for my hour. No, I didn't charge him for his meal. I kept that money all for myself—worker's comp or something, amiright?

Which brings me to today and my job search. Filling out online applications in this job market is kind of awful. Since I can't talk, don't have any kind of work history, and I have no higher education, I'm pretty limited on the kinds of jobs I can do. Busboy at the diner was pretty much the best I could get.

Speaking of the diner. Turns out the owner decided to close it down permanently. Couldn't even give me a reference letter since I worked exactly one hour before walking out. I mean, what was I supposed to do? I wasn't getting paid to clean up blood and bodies.

Maybe I should look into crime scene clean-up. That's not the kind of job that would require me to talk, right?

Because I can't. I don't have vocal cords. Yes, yes. I have a tragic backstory that includes an abusive, narcissistic, surgeon stepfather who removed my voice when I was a colicky baby. Don't worry, I'm not traumatized by it. I was a baby. I don't remember what it was like to be able to scream. Besides, that jerk was killed by the FBI in the first mass murder I witnessed.

I lived the first decade of my life in a cult before the cult leader, the previously mentioned narcissist, decided to kill everyone and start over. The only thing that saved me was the fact that I wouldn't eat or drink anything red, and my stepfather decided to poison us with tomato juice of all things. He was unhinged if he thought ten-year-old Romily Butcher was going to put tomato juice in my pie hole.

"*A Tramp Abroad* by Mark Twain."

I spin in my chair at Mach 3, turning toward the familiar voice behind me. Oh my god. The man! Right there in front of the librarian, still sporting more weapons than any one person should need. Obviously he needs them, but still.

The librarian looks up at the man and arches a brow before handing the man a note. "Careful, Fox. You're the second person to ask for that book today."

The man spins, immediately spotting and completely disregarding me. I mean, I don't blame him. I'm not all that memorable, but still. My hopeful, little, romantic heart gives a twinge at being so easily forgotten.

Ouch, Future Husband. Ouch.

The man disappears down an aisle and out of my life once more, so I turn back to the computer I'm occupying and take up my task again, this time putting headphones on and listening to a YouTube playlist.

I really need a job.

About four applications later, a streak of blood spatter hits my screen, startling the fuck out of me. I rip my headphones off and turn in my chair just in time for a dismembered arm to come flying at me. The thing lands in my lap as my eyes go buggy at the absolute carnage behind me. It's not as bad as the diner, but I don't think the library is going to be able to afford the clean up.

Fighting hand-to-hand with a man at least half a foot taller than him, the love of my life moves whip-quick, battling his opponent for control of a sword. I'm not one to judge, but it just feels strange that anyone would bring a sword to what is obviously a gun fight. Not that my future husband is using his guns at the moment—not the ones that go bang, anyway.

Oh, look at my man go. With a couple of on-point hits, the love of my life manages to disarm the taller dude, grab the sword—

Aaand now there's a head joining the arm in my lap.

Gross.

I push both body parts off my lap and look back up to find my future husband watching me as he catches his breath. I pluck at my blood-soaked shirt and huff. I'm going to have to do laundry now since this was my last clean shirt.

I roll my eyes at the guy and point to my ruined clothes. He glances down at them, and I raise my fingers, rubbing them together to indicate he owes me money for a new outfit. He doesn't, and I let my amused smirk speak for itself. My teasing earns me a small smile before he stalks over to me and hands me another hundred-dollar bill.

I give him a bright smile and that's it. He grabs a book off the floor, shakes the blood off it, and leaves.

Damn that man is fine.

CHAPTER TWO

When a person is as poor as I am, we can make a hundred dollars stretch. Did I buy a new outfit with my hundred dollars? No. No, I did not. I went to a charity closet and replaced my clothes. I saved my two hundred dollars and went home. Well, to the apartment I'm squatting in.

People are all kinds of stupid, and you just have to find the right kind of stupid if you're going to be living hand to mouth. I hung out on the college campus the last month of the semester, listening to students until I found the right person. He has his own apartment, he's all paid up, and he's gone for the entire summer.

Guess who's watering his plants.

I probably should let them die since he didn't arrange for anyone to care for them, but I can't just watch them wither because he's a bit dumb. Plus, it's the least I can do since I'm sleeping in his bed and washing blood-soaked clothes in his washing machine.

On the plus side, no one in this apartment complex has even questioned who I am and why I'm living in his apartment. The neighbors have zero interest in me, and that's perfect. I figure if I can get and keep a job for a few months, I'll be able to afford putting a deposit on a space of my own. Otherwise, I'll have to keep house sitting under the radar.

Oooh! I wonder if there are professional house sitters. I could do that! I wonder how someone gets into that kind of thing. Something to look up at the library today. Thankfully, there are plenty of libraries in this godforsaken city, and the one I went to wasn't even the closest one to the apartment. It was just the biggest one within walking distance. Well, everything is within walking distance considering I walked several hundred miles to get here, but I mean a reasonable walking distance. I don't want to spend hours walking to the library. If I'm going to do that, I'll need some better incentive than shitty internet speeds and old computers.

Since I have some extra cash—thank you, sexy mass murderer—I stop by a food truck run by one of the few men I know who's managed to work himself off the street. His name is Lionel Manchkin, and he's the closest thing I have to a friend.

When I get to the front of the line, Lionel gives me an impassive once over before calling out to the cook behind him. "Manchkin Special!" He shakes his head at me. "Still looking for a job?"

I nod and shrug and hand over five dollars.

He hands me back two dollars and two quarters. "I heard about the diner. They said there were two survivors."

I nod again, point to me and point to the cook behind him.

"You and the cook. You're one lucky bastard."

I shrug again. I am pretty lucky, but I don't think Lionel knows how lucky I am, and if he did, I don't think he would agree.

"I might have an opening for an overnight detailer coming up. Come back to me if you haven't found a job in a week. I'm one write up away from firing my current guy."

I nod again and take the egg, bacon, and cheese sandwich he hands me before slipping away. For two dollars and fifty cents, Lionel gave me three pieces of toast, four eggs, two slices of cheese and four pieces of bacon. It's the sandwich that only Lionel can order for someone, and he only lets his friends have it. It's nothing special except that it's a lot of food for cheap, but it's sometimes the only food I can afford for the day, and Lionel knows that. He doesn't give anything away for free, but he makes the burden of homelessness less burdensome by providing food to some of his old friends.

I eat half the sandwich and wrap up the other half before getting on the subway. One of the few things I pay for is a monthly pass. I might be able to walk all over the city, but it's not feasible if I really want to get out of the gutter. I have to be able to move if I want to keep my prospects open.

"Don't do it."

Holymotherfuckingshit.

I look up so fast, I'm pretty sure I give myself whiplash. The guy is on the subway! Future husband! But maybe this isn't the best thing, because now I'm looking around and almost everyone in this car has a weapon out and they're all staring at my man. Dammit.

I should probably be worried about why so many people are trying to kill this guy, but I'm wearing my *nice* shirt, and I still have half a sandwich left, and I'm pretty sure my man is probably going to kill me too because once is coincidence, twice is suspicious, but meeting three times like this is downright proof that I'm probably someone he should kill. I mean, in his head, not in mine. I'm totally an innocent bystander with bad luck (or is it good luck?), but if I were him, I'd probably kill me on principle.

Especially since I can't defend myself.

Since no one is paying me any never mind, I scoot over the seats and into the furthest corner I can find, curling into a ball with my arms over my head in case of falling body parts.

"Santanos wants you dead, Fox. It's our job to make sure Santanos gets what Santanos wants."

I guess my future husband's name or moniker is Fox since that's the second person to call him that. Fitting. The man is a total fox. Not a silver fox yet, he needs a few years for the silver to start coming into his dark hair, but I can totally see him as a sexy silver fox in about a decade, and I'm so here for that.

Ugh. Closed-box gunshots are deafening. Since I'm already mute and don't want to lose my hearing, I plug my ears with my middle fingers, keeping my arms crossed over my head. Yay for the preservation of my hearing, boo for getting startled by the deadweight of a body that falls on top of me.

I'd complain, but I don't have a voice, so I can't.

When the gunfire stops, I push the body off me and scowl at the blood pooled on the paper covering my sandwich. I huff my annoyance and look up to find Fox looking at me with his head cocked. I hold up my food and point to the blood ruining it before chucking it at the man in a fit.

Honestly, why are so many people trying to kill him?

He doesn't even try to duck the projectile. He just let's it hit him in the leg—yeah, I do *not* have a throwing arm.

I stand up and check my clothes, unsurprised to find them in ruins again and sigh as the train starts slowing down for the next stop. Looking around at the bodies I hang my head and shake my fist at Fox. If he weren't the love of my life, I'd be a bit more piqued, but I guess I'm just glad he's alive.

A hand closes around my fist, making me gasp as I look up, remembering too late that three times is definitely reason enough to kill me. Locking eyes with the man's dark hazel orbs, I'm surprised to find curiosity rather than murder in them.

The relief that he's not going to kill me brings a huge smile to my face. I pat his sticky chest with my free hand, pulling it away bloody. I mean, we're both pretty gross, but when I look at where I patted, I can see a hole in the fabric and think maybe my love has been shot.

I widen my eyes and look up at him, projecting concern. For a brief moment he looks surprised before suddenly he's pulling me out of the subway car, onto the landing, and pushing us through the crowd of onlookers who've stopped to gawk at the gore.

No one even tries to stop him from kidnapping me. Yep. Those fuckers just let the guy pull me right out of the station and onto the street. He hails a cab, and before I've even processed what is happening, because ohmyfuckinggod he grabbed me and my arm is all tingly, Fox is holding my face and looking deep into my eyes like he's as in love with me as I am with him.

"Address?"

Huh?

"What's your address?"

Oh. Dammit. Now the awkward part where I have to figure out how to communicate while being mute and unable to write. I can type, don't get me wrong. I can read and type, obviously; I use the internet all the time, but I never learned to actually write my letters, so…

Also, I guess our love connection is totally one-sided. Not that I blame the man; he doesn't know what a catch I am yet. He's been the one doing all the mating dance stuff, and I've just been watching from the sidelines like a mook.

"Address, Mr. Fox?" the cabbie asks while stupidly taking his life into his own hands.

I widen my eyes at the gun the man pulls and points at Fox, who immediately breaks the guy's arm by bending it in ways it should not go, takes the gun, and stabs the cabbie with a knife that appears out of the air like magic.

Well, that fixes the problem with having to tell him my address.

"Address?" Fox asks again as he gets out of the cab.

Never mind; the problem is not fixed.

I watch in awe as he pulls the cabbie out of the car and then sits in the driver's seat. So this is happening. Yay.

The best thing I can say about the whole cameras in cars thing is that it makes it really easy to type my address into the GPS directions thing. I don't even have to try to explain to my future husband why I can't answer his question. Love it.

Fox doesn't waste time or words; he follows the directions, passes my apartment complex, and parks at the back of a grocery store about five blocks away. Since I walk to this grocery store occasionally, I don't mind the distance and figure he probably parked this far out so that no one would know where to look for my body if he's going to kill me.

I don't think he is.

I have no reason not to think so, but I trust my gut, and my gut tells me we're going to have a long and sexy love affair, not that he's going to kill me for having really bad luck.

I scoot my ass out of the backseat of the cab and turn my best smile on Fox, pointing to the grocery store since I have zero food in my apartment. Not *my* apartment, but you know what I mean.

He glances down at my bloody clothes and then to the grocery store, so I shrug to let him know that no one is going to care we're covered in blood. They'll probably assume it's a flash mob thing or something.

Since he doesn't object, I take his hand—I'm totally willing to risk death for some hand-holding—and lead him into the store. It's the guns and ammo that cinches it for us. We get a lot of looks, but mostly they're amused, because normal people just can't imagine that someone would seriously tote around this many guns and this much ammo, and they certainly assume that anyone covered in blood wouldn't go out in public like that. Obviously it's fake, because we're in a public place acting like we've done nothing wrong.

I mean, *I* haven't done anything wrong, except maybe now I'm aiding and abetting, but that's just how the cookie crumbles when the love of your life is so good at killing people. Grabbing a buggy, I push it one handed, because why would I ever let go of my future husband's hand if I don't have to? I walk Fox through the store, gathering food, a couple of first aid kits, and other things that could be useful if he expects to not get a blood infection from being shot. Yes, I assume he's been shot since there's at least one hole in his clothes.

After making sure I can carry everything, I unload the items into the self-checkout, and then point to the screen when it demands payment, giving Fox my expectant eyebrows.

Half of Fox's mouth turns up in a smile as he shakes his head and pulls out a hundred-dollar bill and feeds it into the machine.

I pat his arm to let him know he's a good man, then grab our stuff in one hand—yes, it's heavy; no, I'm not letting the injured man carry it along with his hundred pounds of weapons—and lead him outside, walking back to the apartments while holding his hand again.

Yeah no, I won't be letting go any time soon.

CHAPTER THREE

Watching Fox tend his wounds is a little surreal. Turns out, he does not have any bullet holes in his body. I know because I didn't even attempt not to gawk when he stripped down to his skivvies. I'm not sure he noticed that I was watching, because even though he has zero bullet holes in him, apparently he got into a fight with a carving knife recently. Well, it was probably a sword, but still, those cuts are deep and the scars will be vicious.

Not that adding a few more scars is going to take away from his beauty. The man is—let me just get a napkin for my drool—*lithe*. Lots of yummy muscles, but nothing over the top. He's not showing his bulk off; he's using his body to be fast and precise. He's got plenty of scarring already and a few scary tattoos. Scary like they look like he got them because he was in the mafia or is in the mafia or something. Though I suspect if he's got mobs of criminals trying to kill him, he's probably on the outs with his organization.

Also, the love of my life doesn't only carry weapons and ammo on him; he also pulled out a surgical needle and thread from his pocket and a human staple gun. He's used both on himself without anesthesia since sitting down at the kitchen table. I don't think he feels pain the way I do because I sure as hell could not stick a needle into my skin without at least flinching, and I flinched for him every time the stapler made its *ktchk* noise.

Since he's done now with tending his wounds, and because it's about food time anyway, I pull out the small pack of ground beef he bought and start prepping the vegetables for spaghetti with meat and vegetable sauce. It's a cheap way to get all the food pyramid into my belly if I count tomato and eggplant as vegetables (I do).

I guess since I spent the last couple of hours gawking at him, it's his turn, and he definitely takes it, watching me like a hawk as I dice up the onion, eggplant, and chop up the mushrooms. The meat browns while the water boils, and I dump the *whole wheat* pasta I bought into the water. I'm not really health conscious, but I do have to be conscious of my nutrient intake since I don't always get nutritious food. So even though I don't really like whole wheat pasta, I eat it because it's got more of the stuff my body needs to be healthy than plain ol' pasta has.

When the food is done, I divide it into four portions and serve two of them on plates. The other two go into the freezer in freezer bags for the next time I need to avoid scurvy. Yes, that's a thing. Yes, I have in fact gotten it once. No, I'm not going to explain how, because it's too embarrassing to contemplate.

Ok, fine, I went through a period of time when I refused to eat anything but bacon. It was not a good choice, but since my foster parents didn't want to be accused of starving me, I ate nothing but bacon for just long enough to get scurvy. After that, I had to go to some nutrition classes and therapy. I'm happy to report I will never not get enough vitamin C again.

Sitting across from Fox, I watch him and he watches me, and then I realize that with all the people out to kill him he's probably wondering if I've poisoned his food, so I take a bite of mine and then take a bite of his and give him another bright smile because he should have more smiles in his life, especially if they're mine since we're going to get married someday.

Fox gives me a small smile back and digs into his food, eating efficiently. There is no indication that he *likes* the food; he's just putting energy into his body. Good thing I tend to cook the more nutritious choices rather than the more delicious choices, because from the way he eats, Fox does not care at all about the taste. Le sigh. I could have used a compliment or two, but I'm just going to appreciate the smile and assume that *good-enough-to-eat* is praise.

After we finish, I wash the dishes while Fox continues to stare at me. Little butterflies of excitement wriggle through me at being under his microscope. The dryer buzzes while I'm contemplating how long before I can get my first kiss from him, so I finish my task and pull our laundry out of the machine. Mine will never be wearable again, but since his is black, the stains don't really show through.

Damn. I guess he's going to cover all his deliciousness again.

I fold up his clothes and mine, grab the stack, and nod my head toward the hallway. If he's going to be putting on clean clothes, he should probably shower off all the leftover blood.

Hmmm, I wonder if he needs help washing his back…

Fox follows me to the bathroom where I put his clothes on the counter and hand him one of my host's nice, fluffy towels. I give him a very seductive once over and sigh when he doesn't invite me to shower with him or at least watch.

Fox's expression doesn't give much away; he's a stoic type of man, so I release a longing sigh and leave him in the bathroom alone. The shower starts running as I put my clean clothes in the basket I've commandeered for my stuff.

Grabbing the book I've been reading, I make a cup of fancy tea from my host's stash and settle in on the sofa to wait for Fox to re-emerge. Communication barriers are a bitch, but my text-to-speech device was stolen three months ago, and those things aren't cheap. Hence why it was stolen.

I guess I could practice my letters instead of reading about gay pirates pillaging the tightest holes on the high seas…but gay pirates are way more interesting than wobbly script written by a guy who can't tell if he's right or left-handed.

No really. I use both hands equally, but holding a pencil never felt right in either hand. You'd think that using eating utensils would clear things up for me, but I use a fork in my right and a spoon with my left and switching them up isn't comfortable. I'm a two-handed eater.

Fox startles me out of my thoughts when he lifts my feet off the sofa and sits, setting them in his lap. I smile happily at the intimacy of the position. Fox's mouth makes an effort to leak his happiness too, but the man squashes the smile almost as soon as it appears.

"What's your name?" he asks, moving his hands in a recognizable pattern.

Yeah, I probably should have learned sign language ages ago, but I've had a text-to-speech device since the government took over raising me, so I never did learn.

Instead of trying to explain the futility of signing to me, I stand up, grab my wallet from the counter, and show him my government issued ID.

"Romily Butcher. You'll be twenty-two on Christmas Day." He hands me back my ID and looks me over. "You're not deaf?"

I shake my head and lift my chin, showing him the surgical scar. It's barely there, hardly noticeable since I was a baby at the time of the incision. Most people don't realize what the small scar means, but my future husband's face darkens when he sees it.

"How old were you when you lost your voice?"

I shrug, hold up two fingers and then mime rocking a baby.

"Two years old?"

I shake my head.

"Two *months* old?"

I nod and shrug. It's not like I remember what life was like when I could vocalize, but the look of sheer indignation on his face makes me squirm happily. I've gotten that look before, of course—most decent people agree that taking a baby's voice is inhumane—but coming from him, it just feels like it means something more than it ever has before.

A knock on the door interrupts my happiness, replacing it with confusion. I put my finger to my mouth and turn just to look at the door. After another moment, the person knocks on the other side. "Open up, Elijah! I know you're in there. We need to talk."

I widen my eyes at Fox, continuing to hold my finger to my mouth. Elijah is the guy that holds the lease on the apartment. The guy talking through the door worries me, since everyone who knows Elijah knows he's in Italy for the summer.

"Come on, Elijah. We both know you came back early because of me. Let's just talk."

Oh no, this is starting to sound like a lover's quarrel. Fuckityfuck. Standing, I walk quietly to the door to check the locks. "Come on, baby. Just open the door."

Shaking my head, I silently attach the chain since I forgot to slide it into place when Fox and I got here. Being the expert that I am in silence, I don't make a sound.

"I saw you, Elijah. You brought a guy home, but I forgive you. He can just leave, and there won't be any hard feelings. You know you'd rather have me. Just let me in. I'll make sure you're taken care of, baby."

Ugh, this guy. I've never had a relationship, but even I can see the red flags. I turn to Fox and roll my eyes, shaking my head.

Bam!

The bang on the door startles me, but obviously I don't make a sound.

"Let me in! I'm not going to let you sleep around like this. You're mine!"

The guy on the other side starts wiggling the door handle, and if I was Elijah I'd be calling the cops, but since I'm not exactly legally living here, I just scoot away from the door and unabashedly hide behind Fox.

The banging continues along with several verbal threats before abruptly ending after about ten minutes. Dude really wanted to get his hands on Elijah, and I'm thinking that my host should probably know his ex is a stalker and he needs a restraining order against him. I'll print off a note for the guy before I vacate. That just seems polite.

When it sounds like the dude is gone, I stand up from where I crouched behind Fox and wipe my hands on my leggings. Yes, I did in fact choose the leggings so that if I got an erection Fox wouldn't miss it and would know I'm so very onboard with some horizontal tango. What? Some people have to use alternate forms of communication because we can't give verbal consent.

Since I should probably explain that we're currently squatting, I fast walk to the kitchen where Elijah Penn keeps his lease in a drawer. I pull it out, showing Fox the lease and pointing to the name. I point to myself and execute a beautiful squat before standing up with a not-so-innocent grin.

Fox stares at me with a blank look then the realization hits him, and he dips his chin with just the smallest impression of an amused smile on his lips. "You're squatting here."

I nod, brightening my smile and returning the contract to its place.

When I return to the couch, instead of sitting where I was, I sit in Fox's lap, wrapping one arm around his neck and pointing to my mouth with the other, puckering my lips. I don't know a better way of communicating my need for kisses, and I'm pretty sure it would have worked, too, except that the sound of someone messing with the front door handle draws our attention away from our first kiss. Before I can react, the knob turns and the door bangs open, stopped only by the chain.

"Open the door before I break it down!" the dude from earlier shouts through the crack.

Fox deposits me on the couch, picks up a gun from the coffee table in front of us, and walks to the door, breaking the chain by yanking the door open. He points the gun at a jock-dude's face. "Come on in," Fox orders as the jock-dude's fear makes an appearance.

With his hands in the air, jock-dude stammers an apology as he comes into the apartment. "I-I-I'm Elijah's boyfriend. Elijah, tell this guy I'm—" His eyes fall on me where I'm standing as far from him as possible. "You're not Elijah."

"House-sitter," Fox deadpans.

The jock-dude swallows hard, eyeing the guns on the coffee table and then the one pointed at him. "I sh-should g-go," he decides.

Fox nods. "Yeah. *Do not* come back."

Jock-dude nods vigorously and scrambles for the door, making a quick exit.

Fox shuts the door behind him and pulls out his phone. Whatever he sees there makes one of his eyes twitch, then he looks up at me, face clear of emotions. "Want a job?" he asks, like maybe he's not sure if this is a good idea or not.

I huff and roll my eyes, putting my fist on my hip. Obviously I need a job. I lost the last one because of him. Not that I blame him. I roll my hand, indicating for him to go on.

Fox almost smiles again. "Don't sass me," he teases, but immediately drops that tone in favor of what I decide is his professional one. "The job is called Harbinger. You announce my arrival. I send you ahead of me as a warning that I'm coming."

I drop my jaw and give him my most incredulous look—I'm really accomplished with nonverbal communication in case that wasn't clear.

"Trust me. You get paid per job. Two grand each time. I'm fairly busy." He looks up at the ceiling for a moment. "My last day off was three weeks ago."

I clear the incredulity off my face and give him a skeptical eyebrow, standing with both fists on my hips.

He cracks a smile and smothers it. "Let's go get you outfitted."

I huff and shake my head giving him an amused smile and letting my laughter shine in my eyes. I guess I'm going to be Fox's Harbinger, whatever that means.

CHAPTER FOUR

Fox is a man on a mission, and his resolute way of shopping made me feel more important and more powerful than anything I'd experienced in my life. Our first stop on Fox's agenda had been a stylist, who took one look at my curly blond hair and gave me a side part by shaving a line for it. He cut the sides and back close and scrunched my curls to the right. He finished my hair, and the next person to touch me was a make-up artist who had given me a natural look that smoothed out my peachy complexion and had used eyeliner to make my brown eyes look huge.

The next stop had been a suit shop where Fox put me in a ridiculously comfortable, brown three-piece suit with a gold brocade vest and a matching silk pocket thing. You know, that pocket thing that's for decoration. He bought me four different suits in the same style, but I had worn the brown one out. Instead of putting me in toe-pinching dress shoes, though, we had stopped at a shoe shop, and he put me in black combat boots, because that totally matches the fancy suits, right? He also bought me some dress shoes but insisted I wear the combat boots out of the store.

As we hit the street out of the shoe shop, Fox poses me against a white wall and takes a full body picture of me. A few screen taps later, that picture is sent via text message to a five-digit number and an automated response comes back, which he shows me:

Thank you for updating your status. Your Harbinger will be announced in fifteen minutes.

After I read that, Fox looks down the street both ways then turns to me, jerking his head for me to follow.

I do and end up walking into a brightly lit modern boutique where a woman dressed as fancy as I am greets us with a customer-service smile. "Good evening, Mr. Fox. How can I be of service today?"

"My Harbinger needs a phone," he replies stoically.

The woman's eyes widen briefly before she closes off her surprise and gives him a deferential bow. "Please give me a moment."

Fox says nothing, and since I can't speak, I don't either, and she takes our silence as confirmation. Turning on her spiked heels, she disappears into the back wall—it's like the openings in the walls of the labyrinth of the Goblin King; you can't tell it's there until you see someone disappear into it. Looking around at the mostly empty boutique, I clock two other women showing phones to customers, and one woman staring at us from behind the cash desk. That one looks at me with keen interest in her Botox-frozen face.

With the subtlety that comes from hiding most of my life, I nudge Fox to draw his attention to the woman staring at me. There's no way I'm dumb enough to get involved with a man known for his ability to murder people in groups and not make him aware of the people giving me too much attention. I'm basically his responsibility at this point. I'll bring joy to his deadly life and he will protect me, and that's a totally fair exchange.

"This place is safe. There are rules, and no one breaks them unless they want a visit from me," Fox explains without bothering to be subtle about it.

The woman cocks her head to the side. "I'm merely curious about why Fox would hire a Harbinger after a decade."

I don't have an answer for her and couldn't say even if I did. Snicker. I love mute puns, but only when I make them.

Fox doesn't deign to answer, and then the woman helping us comes back with a sleek phone, displaying it and then giving us the rundown of all its features—to be honest, I don't listen to anything beyond how to send text messages and answer phone calls. She doesn't bother going over the accessibility options because most people just don't consider people might have unseen disabilities. I'm not offended; I'm sure Google can teach me how to use the phone if I can't figure it out myself.

Fox pays for the phone by giving the woman the back of his hand and letting her scan it. I eye the transaction and wait until we're back on the street before picking up his wrist and pointing at the back of his hand with wide, questioning eyes.

Fox glances between my expression and his hand. "I work for an organization that utilizes chip implants for commerce. You'll get one after a trial period if you choose to remain in my employ."

Well, that's not a conspiracy theorist's wet dream. Nope. Not at all. I give Fox an exaggerated side-eye and shake my head.

"Just because you're paranoid, doesn't mean they're not out to get you," he teases me as I lace my fingers through his.

I haven't had the chance to hold his hand since this morning, and I'm hungry, so he's going to buy me dinner at a sit-down restaurant. Using my new phone one handed, I find a restaurant that won't kick him out for wearing less than formal clothes and start pulling him toward it. It's only seven blocks away.

He comes with me without a word, which is nice. Some people feel the need to fill the absence of my voice with theirs, but I've never needed that. I enjoy people watching, and this city has more than enough people to keep me entertained. Of course, with the disparity of our outfits, we get more than a few double takes. I probably look like his sugar daddy, which makes me huff with delight.

At my silent laughter, Fox looks down at me with a question in his eyes. I indicate my outfit and his and look around us at the people giving us looks. He follows my eyes and releases his own amused huff.

"I'm not calling you 'Daddy,'" he murmurs, barely audible.

I give him my brightest smile, squeezing his hand—I love a man who gets me. Oooh! I have a phone now!

I hold it up and open the contacts, finding "Arlington Fox" already programmed in. With a smirk on my face, I rename the contact "Future Husband," giggling internally. I can't wait to see what Fox thinks of that.

When I look up, he's staring ahead with a small smile on his face pretending that he didn't see me change the contact name. I pocket the phone and hold my hand out to his, making grabby hands.

Fox shakes his head, but hands me his phone. When I find my contact information, it's under the title "Harbinger." I raise a questioning brow at him.

"Automatic update. As soon as the depot got your information, your contact was added to my list," he explains.

I didn't know phones could do that, but I'm also dealing with some kind of criminal organization, so I roll with it. No sense in being surprised when the Illuminati do mysterious shit, amiright?

I edit the contact name to add "aka Future Husband" and give him back his phone. Don't want him to forget he's going to eventually want to buy me jewelry to go with my outfits. Diamonds are this boy's best friend.

Fox glances at the change and shoots me a sexy smirk before pocketing the phone.

Oh yeah, I like a man who can get on the same page as me without a fight.

CHAPTER FIVE

"Hello, I'm Roxanne, can I start you off with a bottle of wine?"

Our server smiles politely, holding her writing pad in front of her tuxedo shirt. Her bow tie sits a little crooked above the generous swell of her bosom, and her teeth have a little red lipstick on them, but she looks like it won't be a fight to get served by her.

"The house wine is fine," Fox says. "And we'll take a sampler appetizer."

She gives us both another polite smile and assures us she'll be back shortly.

I peruse the menu, deciding on a chicken dish that looks edible, and set it aside, looking up to find Fox studying me. I cock my head curiously, silently asking what he's thinking.

He studies me for another few seconds before speaking quietly. "I'm trying to decide why you've never been afraid of me and what kind of person pushes a severed head off their lap before demanding money for clothes."

I snort and roll my eyes as I start typing on my phone, handing it over when I finish. I don't know if his organization tracks text messages, but if I don't have to send personal information out into the ether that is radio waves, I won't. At least, not until I know who's who and what's what.

I grew up in a cult that was murdered by the leader when I was ten. Then one of the boys in one of the homes I was in when I was seventeen decided to kill everyone who ever picked on him. Obviously I'd never teased him aloud, so I wasn't one of his targets. He killed fifteen kids and five adults before offing himself. So I already had two massacres under my belt when you showed up to the diner.

And, why would I be afraid of you? You're competent. You're not going to *accidentally* kill me.

Fox reads my words and hands back my phone. I erase the message while he comes up with a response. "True."

I huff a laugh that the only part of that he can respond to is my last statement.

Plus, I've read that it's almost impossible to kill your fated mate, so I'm pretty confident I'm safe from you.

I hand that over to him and get the gift of an amused chuff of laughter before he cuts it off, glancing at me as he slides the phone back to me and sips his water. "I don't think humans have fated mates."

I fan my hand and roll my wrist, presenting my own face as an example of a human with a fated mate. My teasing smirk draws another huff of laughter from him, but all the joy bouncing between us snuffs out when a man steps up to our table, setting wine glasses on the table and uncorking a bottle.

"Good evening, Mr. Fox. Welcome to Sybillant. If there's anything I can do for you, please don't hesitate to ask." The man pours Fox's wine and turns his almost black eyes on me, making me feel cold with the lack of anything remotely human in them. "And you, Harbinger, welcome. I am Saxon Sybil. Should you ever need my assistance, please do not hesitate to ask. I've instructed the depot to add my contact information to your phone."

That's rather presumptuous of the man. I purse my lips in displeasure and cover my wine glass.

Saxon laughs quietly and gives me a respectful nod. "Best to keep your wits about you when you're involved with Mr. Fox."

He gives us both a quick bow, sets the bottle on the table, and bids us a good evening before leaving again.

I arch my brow at Fox and send Saxon's back a side-eye, telling him I don't trust that guy and that he was creepy as fuck with one expression.

Fox sips his wine to hide his smile and gives me the barest nod, tapping the table.

I push my phone to him and a few moments later, he pushes it back with a message.

The restaurant is safe, but Saxon is a last resort kind of contact. He will take your soul as soon as help you.

That sounds ominous, and honestly a little too on the nose, if you know what I mean. I mean, the guy's eyes were totally dead. I could easily believe in demons after meeting him. I've heard rumors of people who aren't people making appearances in the places where the homeless shelter, but this is the first time I've ever been tempted to believe in demons. Saxon just inspires that kind of paradigm shift.

While I'm considering this, Roxanne arrives with a platter full of a variety of foods. Like, there's more food here than I can eat in a day, but that doesn't stop her from taking out her writing pad as soon as the appetizer is set up and asking if we've decided on our entrees.

Fox orders a steak and then I have to decide if I want to lug a bunch of leftovers around or if I'm content with the appetizer. Greed wins out, so I point to the chicken on the menu and then to the side dishes that look good, and Roxanne disappears with our menus and an assurance she will have our food out as soon as possible.

I watch Fox sip his wine, enjoying the bob of his Adam's apple and the way the dark scruff on his face makes him look like more of a hobo than I am. No, he doesn't get to look distinguished with his scruff; he looks like he could use a shave and a haircut. Like I said, he's not exactly handsome, more like he's an average joe kind of guy and with the day-old scruff he's definitely looking haggard. It doesn't help that he's wearing a bloodstained T-shirt and workout pants.

"Restrictive clothing isn't an option for me," he tells me quietly.

Plus, I know what he spent on my suits; he would be poorer than me in just a few days if he had to buy a new suit every time he worked.

I tap out a few sentences into my phone and slide it to him.

The hobo look isn't sexy, but your confidence is. I'd do you. I'd do you for the rest of our lives.

When he looks up, I wag my brows suggestively and he rewards my bad behavior with another huff of laughter. He types his response under mine and slides the phone back.

Don't let anyone know you're both sassy and crazy. Harbingers have a reputation to uphold.

I cock my head at him, curious what my reputation is supposed to be.

He gives me the barest hint of a mysterious smile and sips his wine, deciding to keep me in the dark because there's no way he misunderstood my nonverbal query.

What's life without a little mystery? I'll find out eventually.

Our server delivers our food, and we eat without filling the time with conversation. I enjoy my food, and his appears to be adequate. He drinks the entire bottle of wine and pays with his subdermal chip, then we're back out on the street and darkness has fallen.

"First job is in a church. All you have to do is go in and walk to the front and sit in the first pew. That is the entirety of your job. We will leave together," he says, hailing a cab.

He pushes me into it, but doesn't get in with me, giving the cabbie the address before shutting me in without so much as a good luck.

Oh well, when you decide to fall in love with a stoic man, you can't expect him to be anything other than stoic. As the cab pulls back into traffic, I give him an affectionate smile through the window—*I'm* not a stoic man, so I don't have to pretend I don't like him.

The drive to the church takes an hour—I could have gotten there on foot faster—but when I pull out cash to pay, the cabbie waves it away. "Harbingers ride for free," he says by way of explanation, smiling a crooked smile and peering at me through startling emerald eyes. He's scruffy but not unkempt like Fox, handsome, and looks friendly, though there's something about him that makes me feel a bit like prey.

I trust my gut, accepting that it's warning me about him but not making me think I'm actually a target. It's odd that I don't have to pay for the ride, but since I'm not one to look a gift horse in the mouth, I get out and walk into the church with my back straight and head held high. I might not be a rich wanker, but I sure can act like it when I'm wearing the right clothes.

Inside, the candles burn on an altar across from the door, and the place has that burned-wax-and-cold-stone smell of old cathedral churches. A surprising number of people litter the pews while a priest stands at the pulpit, though he doesn't seem to be conducting a service. It doesn't much matter anyway, I have one job to do, so I walk with confidence to the front of the church, never faltering even when every head turns as I pass. The very front pew is actually behind the pulpit and to the left, so I walk up the steps past the priest and turn, sitting to face the sanctuary at the very front of the church.

Two elderly men and a middle-aged woman exit the church as the rest of the people stand up, drawing their guns. No one points a weapon at me, but the priest turns to face me.

"May I ask for whom the bell tolls?" He looks…concerned.

Since I don't know and I couldn't tell him if I did, I stare impassively for long enough to make him shift uncomfortably, and then I turn my eyes back to the people awaiting death. I mean, I assume Fox is going to kill anyone who threatens him.

The priest shuffles a bit. "Most Harbingers announce the subject of the contract before the arrival of the Reaper."

I flick my gaze to him, but otherwise ignore him. I mean, I'm not going to tell him I don't know what I'm doing, and I'm not sure I want him to know I'm mute either. Plus, it's kind of fun watching him squirm.

Ten minutes later, Fox slams into the church, wielding a sword. This is clearly a gun fight, and my man brought a fucking sword. He also brought all his guns, but c'mon, *a sword!*

He points his weapon at the priest and glares at the people aiming their guns at him. The priest backs up from the pulpit, which is when I notice the frightened eyes of a young woman who went missing about a year ago. No one missed her, but I noticed when Eva disappeared; we'd become friendly after she offered me her services and I declined by paying her to keep her hands off me. We weren't besties or anything, but we conversed a few times a month before she disappeared.

Damn. The priest—I assume he's the one who abducted her—has been starving her; she's basically skin and bones, but a year ago, my girl was *thicc*. The haunted look in her eyes and the fact that she doesn't scramble out from under the pulpit as soon as she sees me makes my heart ache for her. She must've been living in hell since she disappeared.

Before I can process much beyond heartache and the stirrings of anger toward the priest, Fox gets to work. Gunshots echo in the church, but very quickly limbs start flying every which way, most no longer attached to their owners. I've paid attention to Fox when he's killing loads of people since the first massacre, but now that I literally have a front row seat, I see what I missed before as I watch the man *move*.

My future husband is *fast*! Not faster than bullets, obviously, but he moves faster than his enemies think, that's for sure. He fights with the confidence born of competence, and I think that throws people off. They're not used to anyone standing on the danger end of the gun and acting like they're not worried. His attitude and skill throw them off their game to their own detriment. Sure, some of them remember to actually fire their guns, but when a cacophony of gunfire doesn't slow down the guy they're aiming for, the individuals and the group as a whole get nervous, shaky, and sloppy.

Fox can bring a sword to a gunfight and win because all the people with guns lose their nerve in the face of his superiority. It's not swagger—the man doesn't have an inflated sense of self—it's skill. And it's sexy as fuck.

I'm embarrassed to admit, watching him cut down the people protecting the priest (who is totally running away, and no I'm not going to stop him. I've done my job, thank you very much), that I have a chubby from seeing my man murder people so efficiently. In a church. God, if ever there was a time for a deity to smite me with lightning...

Since I'm not struck down or given the plague or anything, I take my continued living as a pretty solid argument for my atheism or at least against organized religion.

I mean, the priest kidnapping and holding captive my prostitute friend is also a pretty solid argument against organized religion, but since I happen to know some very nice monks who like me and occasionally feed me, I'm going to sit the vote out on whether deities exist and if religion is an appropriate response.

Once Fox finishes with the protectors, he chases the priest down, jogging past and leaving me with a traumatized Eva and a bunch of dead bodies. I wave at her, inviting her out of her prison with a curl of my fingers.

She flinches at the movement, but then a shadow of the woman who used to work the streets with confidence and sass comes into her eyes and she shakily crawls out from under the pulpit.

I make a crackly noise in my mouth and move my hand across my throat and point at where the priest ran off.

She basically crumbles to the floor in stark relief.

Figuring I don't need to stay in my seat now, I get on the floor with her, pull her head into my lap, and watch her breathe until Fox returns with the head of the priest skewered on his sword. He stabs the pointy end into the pulpit with a loud bang, causing Eva to whimper and curl in on herself at the noise.

He looks down at the woman and then at me with a silent question, so I type out an answer and send it to his phone.

Me: *Do you know anyone who deals with the victims of trafficking crimes?*

Fox reads the message, nods once, and lifts his phone to his ear waiting a moment before speaking. "St. Stephen's church. One in the sanctuary. There may be more stashed in other places."

He ends the call and puts his phone away, looking down at Eva. "Someone is coming to help you. It's in your best interest to let them, but if you're not here when they arrive they aren't going to go looking for you. Your life is in your own hands."

Eva looks up at me, begging with her eyes for something, but as good as I am at reading people, I have no idea what she wants from me.

Gently petting her greasy hair, I exaggerate a sympathetic frown and tip my head to the side to question her for clarification.

"Who's coming for me?" she whispers, darting her eyes toward Fox and widening them.

I pat her shoulder and reach up for Fox's bloody hand, understanding her fear now. He follows my lead and lets me pull him close enough I can kiss the back of his hand. Then I smile up at the man of my dreams and turn that expression down for Eva to see, displaying my affection for him.

She sighs and closes her eyes, accepting that I trust my man. I sure hope whoever he called doesn't break Eva's trust in me.

I continue to hold Fox's hand and pet Eva's hair until three women walk into the church and over to us, completely ignoring the bodies all over the place.

"Fox," the three women say in unison as they come to a stop behind me.

One of them leans over my shoulder, catching Eva's attention. "I'm Gretchen, these are my sisters, Geraldine and Gertie. We run a shelter, and we're here to invite you to come stay with us if you would like to."

Eva swallows her fear, looks at me for a few long moments, and then nods to Gretchen. "I'll come," she whispers, throat raspy from possible dehydration and misuse or disuse; could be either, could be both. Depends on how cruel the priest was and how broken my friend is.

Gretchen makes a happy sound and the next few minutes fly by in a flurry of high energy women taking care of someone in desperate need of their attention. Fox and I walk them out to their van, and then it's just me and him on the street and it's almost midnight.

I look up at him and mime sleep, wondering if he has more plans for the night or if I can go home.

He nods and hails a cab, helping me into the car and following me inside. He gives the cabbie an address in one of the brownstone neighborhoods, and I almost try to cuddle up to him before remembering he's covered in blood and I don't want to stain my nice new suit, so I lean back in my seat and close my eyes until we reach the place we're heading.

CHAPTER SIX

Waking up in the luxury of a memory foam mattress and under a thousand pounds of blankets are life goals I didn't realize I should have had. I'd set my sights on just having a roof over my head; I should have been aiming higher: a bed I never want to get out of.

Even better? The smell of both coffee *and* bacon permeating the air.

Even though I'm absolutely *loath* to leave the bed, the siren call of breakfast pulls me out of my warm cocoon. I almost trip over nothing as I get my bearings, but I manage to make it to the bathroom without taking a header into the floor or a wall or any of the random tables all over the place.

Fox's brownstone is beautiful and clean, and my man has some kind of obsession with tables because there are at *least* five flat surfaces of some kind in every room. Even the hallway has a couple of thin wall tables. The bathroom has one built to sit over the back of the toilet *and* one directly across from it.

Now I'm not one to judge. A man wants to decorate his house with tables, that's his business, but it's not like he *uses* them for anything. They're purely some kind of messed up idea of decoration because he doesn't put anything on them. Not flowerpots, not mail, not even lamps. They just exist in his space.

Ok, it's a weird obsession. I can admit that, but it isn't unlivable. I can learn to live with his strange collection of furniture-mesas. The sacrifices I'd make to ensure the happiness of the love of my life are almost endless. I'd probably stop just short of actual human sacrifice. Probably. I mean, it's not like I have a problem with his profession, so if I suddenly discovered he was killing all those people as a ritual, I might not stop at human sacrifice...

Nah. He doesn't ritually kill people. They attacked him first before he *justifiably* defended himself with extreme prejudice.

As I wander into the kitchen, Fox turns from where he's standing at the stove scrambling eggs into a pan full of sautéed vegetables. He looks me up and down before jerking his head to the coffee pot where an empty cup awaits me next to a carton of half and half.

I tip a bit of the half and half into my cup and then fill the rest with coffee, sipping the brew and sighing because it's definitely the best cup I've ever had. Smooth and robust and everything a cup of coffee should be.

Damn, I'm going to be so spoiled living here. And yes, I am moving in even though Fox and I haven't discussed living arrangements yet. I don't see the point in beating around the bush. I am going to marry the man, and yeah, maybe we haven't even kissed yet, but that is going to happen and then we'll move on to hand jobs and eventually fucking, and between all that physical stuff we'll get to know each other and fall in love, and he'll give me the biggest diamond engagement ring I've ever seen and we'll get married and live happily ever after. So I don't see the point in trying to live apart when we're destined to cohabitate for the rest of our lives.

Sitting at the smaller of the dining tables, the one in the breakfast nook that overlooks the back garden, I watch the birds taking their morning baths in the fountain at the center of the garden. Someone, presumably Fox, has scattered seed in the yard, and a flock of sparrows are enjoying the offering. Along the edges of the tall walls, a cornucopia of food plants thrive, heavy with their bounty. When Fox sets a plate in front of me, I match the vegetables in the scramble to the ones in the garden and sigh happily. Homegrown food is always more flavorful than what grocers get.

Picking up my fork, I point to the garden, then Fox, then my plate and give him my curious expression.

He follows my line of questioning because we're soulmates and he gets me even when the question isn't one hundred percent clear. "It's slightly safer to grow my own food." He pauses, examining me for something. He must find what he's looking for or decides that it doesn't matter. "My property is warded against attack. No one who intends to harm me can cross my property line." He waves at the interior of his home. This isn't a narrow brownstone crushed in with five others just like it; it's been remodeled so that it's a triple wide expanse of space and luxury. "I own the whole building."

Listen, I'm not dumb and I read incessantly because homelessness is boring as fuck and libraries are free. In books, "warded" means magic, and it's clear from the way Fox paused before speaking that he was saying something important. Hence I'm forced to seriously consider the idea that magic and spell craft are something Fox believes in, and being the practical man he is, I very much expect that in about three seconds I'll have to accept that magic is real.

Ok, yeah, that sucks. Paradigm shifts can be painless—my last one was fine—but damn. Jealousy is an ugly thing. And yes, I am absolutely jealous of any and all magic users, because I've spent all of my adult life damn near powerless, homeless, and barely scraping by.

Goddammit.

I sigh and drop my chin to my chest, angry and jealous and maybe a little sad.

"Magic is real," Fox murmurs, proving that his magic is *not* of the psychic variety, since I don't need to be convinced.

I scoff and roll my eyes, and those fuckers betray me by dropping actual tears. Offended by the saline on my cheeks, I dash the droplets away as quickly as possible. Since I didn't bring my phone, I make grabby hands at him.

Fox stares at me in horror, which is the most emotive I've seen him, and it kind of cracks me up. I make the motion of typing on a phone and demand his again. Relief flashes across his face before he gets his expression back under control and slides his phone across the table.

I'm just jealous. I've spent my entire life powerless and if I'd had even a kernel of magical power, I would have had more power than I've ever had.

And that's the truth.

He reads my explanation and then grunts before setting his phone midway between us. "You're not powerless now. Harbingers are…" He pauses as he searches for the right words. "Respected. Untouchable."

I hope that's not literally true, because I have plans to be touched a whole hell of a lot by this man.

He must read my expression because a smirk makes a brief appearance before he hides it behind his coffee cup. "I mean, no one in my world can harm you. Harbingers are protected. You're warded too." My disbelief must show on my face because my normally breviloquent man explains in detail. "Weapons can't touch you; you can't ingest poisons, no one can lay a hand on you who intends harm. You have power now. It's passive, but it's yours."

So, I'm indestructible?

I slide the phone I snatched up to write that back to him.

He nods once. "As long as you're my Harbinger. You'll be able to go back to your life if you choose not to continue after your trial period."

I give him my *as-if* look and smile. This whole magic thing just got a little more awesome.

After breakfast, which is delicious, I shower and dress in one of the suits I find hanging in the closet in my room. Before I fix my hair and try to mimic the make-up from yesterday, I shoot Fox a text.

Me: *At some point, I need to go retrieve my stuff.*

Future Husband: *I'll send someone unless you need to do it yourself.*

Me: *How will they know what belongs to me?*

Future Husband: *Your stuff won't smell like the lessee of the apartment.*

Me: *Valid. Leave Elijah a note warning him that his ex is a stalker and thank him for hosting me. I might have been squatting, but I don't want to be rude.*

Of course, now I'm wondering if he's talking about magic sniffers or actual sniffers like dogs, but you know what? I want to find out on my own. I love a good mystery, and I literally cannot think of anything more mysterious than magic being real. How deep does that go? Are there werewolves? Dragons? Vampires? Demons? Or is it only witchy stuff like spells and incantations? I want to know, but I want to see if I can figure it out without asking too many questions.

Oh, I'll ask, but not outright. It'll be a game. What can I figure out and what do I have to ask about? How many points do I earn if I get something right without asking? Hmm. I think the end game should be fifty points. One point if I'm partially correct, two if I guess right.

This will be fun.

My phone buzzes and I set the eyeliner down to check it.

Depot: *3223 C St. 10:34 am. Cornelius Gavin Stauffer.*

I assume this is my next assignment, so I quickly finish with the eyeliner and head out of the bathroom to the living room where Fox is strapping on his weapons. I put my boots on and check my pocket for my phone and wallet, then turn to him. I have an hour to get to my assignment, but I have no idea what he wants me to do when I get there.

He doesn't pause in arming himself. "You should head out. Take a cab."

That's all he gives me to work with, so I shrug, stride over to him and force him to lean down long enough to kiss his cheek then step back, smiling brightly as I tap my own cheek in expectation.

Fox huffs a breath of laughter and leans down to kiss my cheek. "See you there," he whispers as he pulls away.

I nod my acknowledgement and head out, finding a main street and hailing a cab. The cabbie's green eyes widen in surprise when he turns to look at me, but he doesn't otherwise say anything as I show him the address on my phone. It's the same guy who took me to the church, which is astronomical odds considering the thousands of cabs in this city. My gut is still telling me he's a predator, but not one that's targeting me, so I just pat my belly and let it know that we're alright.

I watch the city slowly pass by as we crawl through traffic during a busy time of day. It takes almost the entire hour to get what amounts to a mile as the bird flies. I could have walked the distance in twenty minutes. Rolling my eyes at the ridiculousness of having to take a cab to my jobs, I pat the cabbie's shoulder in thanks, not even offering to pay; he zeroed out the meter already anyway.

When I get out onto the sidewalk, I'm standing in front of a clothing boutique with evening dresses on the mannequins in the windows. Curious how a clothier managed to get on Fox's radar, I enter the store. Since this is only my second job, I project confidence as I walk over to and behind the cash desk, leaning up against the wall as the woman standing at the register turns wide, frightened eyes on me and runs straight out the door.

Two customers follow her out, leaving me with just one woman eyeing me in confusion and a short man staring at me in terror.

"Who—who—who?" he stammers, but it doesn't really matter, does it?

Fox is only going to kill whoever needs to die.

Wow. I should probably do some belly button staring to figure out where my moral compass went. Who just stands around waiting for someone to come kill a person? Me. That's who. Well, and I guess the lady who's walking toward me with a dress on a hanger. She rounds the cash desk and leans up against the wall with me.

The man stares at us, frozen in place until the bell above the door announces Fox's arrival, then he squeals like a stuck pig and pees himself. Fox barely glances at him, heading into the back of the store. I hear two gunshots then a couple of loud thumps, then Fox comes out, not even a little bloody.

He jerks his head at me, and we exit the store to the soundtrack of the man's whimpers and the woman saying, "Yeah, he's definitely the perfect Harbinger for Fox."

Whatever that means.

Fox stops on the sidewalk and does absolutely nothing for a full minute. Well, he breathes, but otherwise doesn't do anything else. Then he turns to me, studying me again. "You should probably meet Annette," he decides, offering me his hand.

Like I'd ever disabuse him of the notion our hands should always be linked. I thread our fingers together and follow his lead down the street.

We walk for about half an hour at a leisurely pace. At the mouth of an alley, he stops again, cocking his head as if listening for something, then a man slinks out from behind a dumpster, gun trained on Fox. "Santanos requires a face-to-face," the man says almost quietly enough that I can't hear him.

Fox squeezes my hand and drops it, walking into the alley toward the man with a gun. I mean, I've seen him get shot at, and I know I can't be shot, so for a moment I contemplate using my body to protect him, but then I remember that my man has competence in spades, and if he wants me to stand here and do nothing, that's exactly what I'm going to do.

My man gets within a few yards of the dude holding the gun and *moves*.

In microseconds, the gun clatters to the ground behind the Santanos guy and then Fox makes him look at his own ass. Too bad his body can't keep up. The sound of bones breaking is loud even from where I am on the sidewalk.

Fox looks around as the dude's body collapses, but not finding anyone else to kill, he returns to me, taking my hand again. I give him a curious look and make a show of looking behind him. That's the second time I've heard that particular name before Fox killed someone, and I'd like to know who Santanos is and why he *unwisely* wants Fox's attention.

One of Fox's eyes twitches in annoyance. "It's something like a gang rivalry."

I arch a brow at that, almost not believing the utter ridiculousness of that statement.

"Santanos is Annette's opposite. Annette dispenses justice, Santanos makes justice indispensable."

Interesting. Maybe I'll ask Annette a few questions when I meet her. I urge Fox to keep moving, and he leads on without more than a nudge.

Before long we enter a high-rise office building and head up on the elevator to the thirtieth floor. When we step out, we're met with an opaque glass door with a simple sign that tells us we're entering the law office of Annette Killian, LLC.

Fox walks in without a pause, leading me to the paralegal's desk where a nameplate says we're approaching Annie Mallory. She greets us with a smile, but it falls off her face as soon as she realizes who we are. Or rather, who Fox is. "Conference room," she says without preamble as she picks up her phone.

Fox leads me on, down a hall, and through the open door of a cozy study with a long conference table. The shelves are lined with books, and it smells like cigar smoke and book paper, which immediately relaxes me—who doesn't love the smell of fragrant tobacco and books?

Fox takes a seat on one of the sofas away from the table, and then the man pulls me into his lap. I like where this is going. Hand-holding and lap-sitting are totally things we should do. Giving him my happiest smile, I kiss his cheek again, because he should be rewarded when he treats me in the way in which I want to become accustomed.

He suppresses whatever smile I know he wants to give me and squeezes my hip as a woman in a beige suit enters the room and closes the door behind her. She has strawberry blond hair pinned up in a chignon—yes, my uneducated ass knows that word—and pulls a cigar out of a box and lights it before even acknowledging us. She pours herself a tumbler of some dark liquor from a crystal decanter and turns toward us, grinning when she sees me on Fox's lap.

"You must be Romily. Welcome to the family." The way she says that in a smooth whiskey-and-smoke voice makes me think she doesn't actually think of her people as family. She's not exactly a motherly figure, is she? Maybe the crazy cool aunt that drops by on holidays with age-inappropriate gifts for her nieces and nephews. "I'm Annette. You work for Fox. Fox works for me. I work for a council of pricks with sticks shoved so far up their asses that I'm sure all their food tastes like wood and shit. The pricks in question keep the universe from imploding, so we put up with them. Any questions? Fox isn't the best communicator."

I grin, completely in love with this woman. If Fox hadn't found me first, I'd totally tap that. I elbow my man as I pull out my phone and type out my message to her before offering her my phone.

I'm almost sorry that I already decided to marry Fox. I'd be your sugar baby in a heartbeat. Can I call you Daddy anyway?

Annette snorts and laughs hard. "Oh yes. Please do."

God, how is it possible to find two soulmates within a week. I find and immediately change the name of her contact info in my phone to "Daddy."

I'm betting Santanos also works for the council of pricks?

Annette reads my question and hands me back my phone, sitting next to Fox on the sofa and pulling my legs into her lap. "That's right. He's the yang to my yin. Or vice versa. I'm not into that philosophy shit. We both have jobs to do, and we do them under the direction of the council." She takes a long draught of her drink before offering me the tumbler.

I shake my head because I've never learned to like the burn of liquor nor the side effects.

Just so I'm clear, Fox kills people that need killing, and Santanos probably is the reason they need killing?

"I do love a newbie with critical thinking skills," she sighs with a wicked smirk. "There's always someone in need of killing. Not always in the city, though. You'll have to travel too. Your papers will be sent to Fox's home, including your passport. Those will arrive tomorrow, likely. You're going to stick it out, I can tell, so Fox is going to take you to get chipped after this. I'm reducing your trial period. Speak now or forever hold your peace if I've read you wrong."

I shake my head and mime zipping my lips; obviously I'm not giving this new life up.

Can't marry Fox if he thinks I'm going to die because of him.

Obviously being married to a murderer comes with some risks; being indestructible makes those risks negligible.

She laughs again and pats my legs before pushing them off her lap and standing. "Send me the invite to your wedding when you get around to it. I'm so there for that spectacle." She pats Fox's shoulder with clear affection. "Good job, Fox. He's definitely a keeper."

She drains her glass and exits the conference room, which means I should probably get off Fox, but before I do, I wag my brows at him and press my lips to his. I don't deepen the kiss, but I do linger briefly before pulling back.

Fox's expression darkens with desire as I meet his gaze after that intimate exchange. He stares at me without moving until I get to my feet, then he stands, crowding close, and dips down, kissing the corner of my mouth as he entangles our fingers. "Definitely a keeper," he murmurs, watching me with covetous eyes.

Holy hotness. I *love* the way he's looking at me. No one ever has ever looked at me like that before, and I didn't even know what I was missing before now. Possessive alpha type? Yes, please. Sign this mute boy up! Damn, I'm the luckiest man alive, and I know it. I'm going to spend the rest of my life keeping that look in his eyes just to keep feeling like this. Like I'm important. Wanted. Desirable.

Oh, yeah. I'm going to get used to this. Spoil me rotten, Fox, and I'll spoil you. Even if you have a weird obsession with tables.

CHAPTER SEVEN

So, getting chipped is about as awful as it sounds. My hand throbs where it's getting used to having a foreign object shot into it. I've been assured that my body will heal around it and I won't even notice it's there. Oh, and because I'm a Harbinger, I had to do it myself, because I'm the only person who can damage my body, and needle insertion is technically a puncture wound. So that was awful.

On the plus side, I now have access to my paychecks, and I can make cash withdrawals at any bank as long as I ask for the right manager. The right manager always goes by the moniker "Jeeves." I find it hilarious that I'll have to type that out every time I want to carry cash. I have to ask Jeeves for money. It's hilarious.

Fox dumps a load of fresh veg onto the counter next to the sink as I'm taking stock of the contents of his fridge and pantry. I found a deep freezer full of meat in the pantry and everything is very clearly labeled with permanent marker on scotch tape wrapped around paper-wrapped meat. Clearly my man gets his meat in bulk; like he buys beef a cow at a time. Well, I don't know how much meat one gets when one buys a whole cow, but I don't think it would fit in the freezer in his pantry, so maybe he buys a quarter of a cow at a time. Anyway, it's a lot of food to have stored in an appliance that could stop working at any minute.

Why yes, I do think of worst-case scenario shit, because then I can plan for it.

Not that I have a plan for how to save hundreds of pounds of meat when his deep freezer goes out. That's going to take some creative planning. I might have to buy one to keep in a box to replace that one. I wonder if there is such a thing as a cold spell or maybe a works-like-new spell. Things to keep an eye out for…

I jump up on the counter next to Fox and watch him wash the vegetables. I pick up the eggplant and stroke it suggestively, grinning at Fox the entire time. Fox glances up and then does a double-take, which is so comical I nearly fall off the counter laughing. Fortunately for my head, he catches me with his wet hands and keeps me planted on the counter while taking the eggplant away. I pull him between my legs, resting my hands on his shoulders when I've gotten control of myself again.

His amusement ekes out in a small huff of laughter and a smile that makes it to his eyes and sticks around even when his lips relax and his tongue darts out from between them. If that's not an invitation to make out, I don't know what is, so I lean forward and press our lips together again, this time lingering until he takes a hint and opens up.

The first swipe of my tongue against his slays me. He tastes so good, but more than that, he feels like exactly where I belong. Home. I've come home, and I'm never leaving again.

Gripping him hard, I scoot forward as his hands come around to grab my ass as he pulls me flush against him. My breath comes in pants as my heart rate skyrockets, and arousal flushes through me like someone broke a dam and flooded my entire body with all the feel-good hormones I can take. Making out with him, tangling tongues, and just occupying the same space turns me into a soup of melty desire and questionable decision-making skills. I would probably do anything to get the man naked right now, but I haven't actually decided it's time for sex yet, so with a lot of regret and a small amount of pride in my self-control, I pull back to clear my head and lean my forehead on his shoulder.

Fox loosens his grip on me, but I'm not ready for the end of this full-body contact, so I wrap all my limbs around him and squeeze, telling him with my body that he better hold on or there will be consequences. I kiss his neck just under his ear and sigh when he tightens his grip on me and leans into the hug. Oh, yeah, this is lovely. It would be better without clothes, but I don't think I need to rush into getting naked. I've barely managed one make-out with the man. Speaking of, I think I need a bit more sugar before dinner.

I kiss my way along his jaw back to his lips and dive in again, more ready this time for the flood of excitement and pre-sex hormones. It doesn't matter how fuzzy they make me feel or how achingly hard my dick gets, we're going to take this love affair one step at a time, even if that means we have to take breaks between kisses to get ourselves under control.

I really want to rub up on him, but having a plan and keeping to it is one of the things I am good at, so instead of letting the warm, wet, sucking, delicious kisses push me into acting like an omega in heat (yes, I do in fact read all sorts of trashy romance. Why do you ask?), I ease back again and take a break. Lunch would probably be a good way to keep from coming in my pants, but maybe I should go have a private moment in the bedroom first.

Fox kisses my shoulder and up my neck, squeezing my ass in a rhythm that gets me all tingly and makes my body think it's about to get more than a little treat. Shut up, I'm allowed to not put out on the first date.

Not that this is a date. Last night was a date. This is domesticity.

Before I am tempted to rip his shirt off and have at him, I pull myself back and push him away, showing him the need on my face so he knows this isn't a rejection; it's a postponement.

Fox takes minute to clear his own cobwebs before finally realizing that we're not fucking on the kitchen counter, and he squeezes my knees to let me know he understands before going back to the task of washing his vegetables.

I should feel bad that the water's been running this whole time, but I don't. I don't feel even a little bad about being wasteful. In fact, I'm grinning like a lunatic as I hop off the counter and start pulling ingredients for cobb salad out of the fridge. Who keeps bleu cheese on hand just in case? Fox does, that's who.

Soulmates are the best.

CHAPTER EIGHT

I'm not really a TV watcher, so while Fox watches whatever he's into, I lie with my head on his lap reading on my new kindle app. I didn't even have a kindle account until Google explained that I should get Google Play and then told me that kindle had more options. I swear, it's like Google thinks I should give it my money. SMH.

Cozy under the throw Fox covered me with and happy with cuddling like this, I almost wish I could vocally groan when a text from the depot comes in while I'm reading. Apparently, they like to cut it close on deadlines —see what I did there? Puns are awesome—because the address is close enough to walk and I only have fifteen minutes to get there.

I sigh, put my phone in my pocket and stand, grabbing my vest off the back of the couch and buttoning it on, then adding my suit jacket over it and heading for the door where I've decided to utilize one of the entryway tables (there's three) for my shoes. While I pull on my combat boots, Fox starts strapping on his guns and ammo and, oh look at that, he's got another sword out from the ethereal hiding place where he stores his weapons when not in use. No, I don't know that he actually hides them in ethereal dimensions; I just haven't seen where he gets his weapons from since most of them are just sitting out all the time.

He's going to have to learn to use a gun safe when we start having kids. If we start having kids. Honestly, I'm not sure I'm parent material. Husband material? Yeah. I'm so down for marital bliss. Kids? That might be something to talk about in like ten years. Maybe we skip the helpless baby stage and go for adopting middle schoolers. Eh, we've got time to figure it out.

As soon as I get my boots on, I traipse over to him and pull him down for a kiss, marking my territory and saying goodbye before heading out ahead of him. Since it's pretty late now, I hail a cab, and traffic doesn't stop us from getting to the address in a timely manner. In fact, I have a few minutes before I need to walk in, so I wait in the cab, setting a timer so I don't lose track of time as I pull up my book and start reading again. It's a pretty good college nerd/jock romance, and I am all in on whether the game of gay chicken the side characters are playing is going to implode or not. Spoiler alert. It will; that's the next book in the series.

When my timer goes off, the cabbie jumps, making me realize he's probably afraid that my sitting here means that he's the target, but honestly, if he's not doing bad things, he shouldn't be worried about getting a visit from Fox.

I give him a *"really?"* look and get out, wasting zero seconds on trying to comfort the guy. I have an appointment inside what looks like a tattoo parlor. Well, it's a body art shop, and they also do piercings and henna art. Fun. I wonder if anyone will survive, and if they do, if I can get some henna designs. I realize that, in America, they're popularly known to be for brides and special occasions for women, but I don't care about gender roles and would totally rock henna art.

As soon as I walk in, I realize that there's just no hope that I will be able to make an appointment with anyone here. The atmosphere grows heavy and dark while what appears to be a gang of fifteen heavily tattooed skinheads all look at me like I've lost my goddamn mind.

The tension barely shifts as a man the size of a linebacker ducks through a doorway and stops to stare at me. His eyes narrow, and his hand goes to the gun on his hip. "Which one of these fuckers are you looking for, Harbinger?"

Seriously, why does everyone ask? Don't do shit bad enough to get on Fox's list and don't attack him if you see him, and you're not in danger! If I had a voice, I would tell him that, but I don't, so I just take a seat on the arm

JENNIFER CODY

of one of the couches, pull out my phone again, and start reading. I came, I showed myself, I took a seat, and now I get to read until Fox arrives. Since he's been a few minutes behind me the last two times, I can probably get a few pages read. The guys are just about to fuck for the first time, and I really want to know if the jock's going to have a gay freakout. I love gay freakouts. They're hilarious.

Hmmm, this might be another one of those things I should probably navel gaze about: angst in books makes me laugh. I find it utterly ridiculous and laughable, probably because the worst problem the jock has is possible locker room homophobia, and I've lived on the streets for years because I actually had no prospects at all. Jock can still get his college education even if he has to quit the team (he won't because this is *entertainment*), so the angst just makes me laugh because he's not really down by much when he realizes he's gay for the nerd. Not that I know this one will have a gay freakout, I'm just hoping for it.

"Harbinger," the leader guy growls when I don't respond to his question.

I glance up, but seeing as I can't exactly tell him anything at all—and I'm beginning to suspect that's *why* Fox chose me—I turn my nose back to my book.

Fox brings me out of the story just as the nerd gets his third finger shoved into his own hole, so I put my phone away and watch with hearts in my eyes as he points his sword at one of the squirrelly guys on the couch next to me.

That must be Martin, the guy we're here to kill. And since I don't want blood on my suit, I move away from him, walking to the leader when he barks at his men, "Keep it in your pants! Martin's the only one who needs to die tonight."

"No!" Martin squawks, scrambling over the back of the couch to get away from certain doom. I mean, he's not going to get away, but it's interesting to watch the byplay of his thoughts and emotions as he tries to escape his fate.

He manages to get his gun up and a shot off, screaming, "Help me! Don't let him get me!"

The leader barks another disengage order, but only about half of the gang decides to follow his command. The other half decide to help Martin since he did in fact manage to shoot my soon-to-be lover. Not that the bullet so much as slows Fox down.

The blade of Fox's sword glints as he starts moving through the small crowd of skinheads, freeing limbs and heads until everyone who decided to attack him to protect the Martin guy is dead. He marches on to Martin, who shoots him again before losing his hands and then his head in two swift, merciless strokes.

When my man is done with the killing, and I'm sporting a serious boner, I look up to the man I'm standing with and pat his leather vest right over his heart, giving him a sympathetic frown. It's not my *most* sympathetic look, but I feel like I should reserve that for people who don't base their personalities on the things that they hate.

The guy looks down at me, hard eyes glinting with actual fire—oh my god, is he a demon?—and then he looks around at the survivors. "Half our crew died fighting a Reaper, which made them too stupid to live. Don't mourn these fuckers; just bury them and move on. Clean up the mess and start making a list of prospects." He turns to Fox as he places a hand on my shoulder. "Your Harbinger is just like you. Congratulations, Mr. Fox." He sounds almost sincere, so maybe I prejudged these men because they have tattoos instead of hair.

Fox glances at where the guy has his hand on me before looking back to the gang leader. "You will lose that hand, Dante."

Dante immediately removes his hand, and I step away from him, heading to the exit while trying not to slip on the blood and body parts. Tile plus pools of blood; I think I'd have to be wearing non-slip shoes for that to not be a serious hazard to the health of my clothing.

Fox follows me out of the shop and takes my hand as we start walking back home. Normally I'd just let the walk pass in silence, but I really want to know what Dante is, and I am totally guessing demon because of the fire-eyes and association with Santanos.

Is Dante a demon?

"Just an eighth. He's mostly human," he responds quietly.

I give myself one point because I was partially correct. I got the species correct even if I was a few generations off from the truth.

Switching gears completely, I type out a quick note.

We should go on our second date tomorrow because I've decided not to put out until date three, and I might combust if we take too much time getting there.

Fox, my competent, sexy, confident Reaper, shoots me a smirk and pulls me into a dark alcove, leaning up against the wall and pulling me close enough to kiss. "I don't remember taking you on the first date," he hums softly, the movement of his lips whispering against mine.

If he wants to have a conversation with me, he's going to have to learn to give me breathing room and not get me riled up beforehand. I can't just whisper back how the restaurant last night was definitely our first date, so instead I close the miniscule distance between us and push my tongue into his mouth. My brain misfires when I get the coppery taste of blood instead of the flavor he had before lunch. It reminds me that he's been shot a couple of times and I've just ruined my suit by pressing up against him, but then I decide that Fox knows Fox's limits and I can get a new suit, because his hands squeeze my ass and pull me close, and he grinds my cock into his, and I'm about three seconds away from saying fuck it and demanding a sloppy, rushed handjob with this make-out session.

I don't, because I have a plan and self-control, but *ohmyfuckinggod* I want to.

At least I do until Fox being yanked away from me knocks me to the ground. I hit my head pretty hard, but the invisible force that keeps me protected from harm makes it so that I don't even feel my head bounce off the sidewalk. I scramble to my hands and knees as four people, all sporting pink mohawks, wrap Fox up in chicken wire, which causes him to smoke everywhere it touches his skin.

I launch myself at the nearest one, pissed that they interrupted an amazing makeout session. I'm not a trained fighter, but I can scrap with the best of the street kids, and I take out all my frustration on the guy I land on, pulling his head back by his mohawk and punching him in the neck, fully intent on breaking his hyoid. I have zero interest in a fair fight, so as soon as he starts choking, I grab the next person, a chick with some amazing wings around her eyes, and pull her away from Fox, punching her as hard as I can in the neck too.

I don't even know why Hollywood tries to sell fights with people hitting each other in the head. I have no desire to break my hand on some fucker's skull, and hitting people in the neck is a great way to cause a ruckus in their body. Coughing and choking tend to keep people from being able to effectively fight back.

I turn to grab the next one but find Fox standing over two headless corpses with his phone next to his ear. He jerks his chin for me to get behind him, and I do because I didn't kill my two. I mean, they're going to die, and if I broke their hyoids it's possible they'll die because of what I did, but they're not dead *yet*.

At least not until Fox swings his sword twice and alleviates them both of the burden of their heads.

Maybe I should take up yoga. Isn't yoga the meditation exercise that helps people become better humans? I should look into that; I'm beginning to think I might have a kink for watching my man work, and if he was a baseball player, that would make sense, but since he's apparently a *Reaper*, that's probably something I should talk to a therapist about.

Not that I would be caught dead talking to another therapist. Fuck that. I've had more than my fair share of couch time. Not that I think other people shouldn't have therapists. Other people definitely should. In fact, I would say almost every person I've ever known would have benefited from some therapy…

Ok, back to Fox talking on the phone, because that's more important than my thoughts on therapy for humans.

"If the council doesn't want Santanos dead, they need to call him off me."

That's all he says, then he hands me the phone and I put it to my ear, clicking my tongue because it seems polite to let whoever I'm not talking to know that I can hear them.

"Sugar baby! I assume that's you clicking at me. Click once for yes and two for no."

I click once, grinning at the sound of Annette's voice.

"Are you hurt?"

That's a dumb question, but I click twice anyway.

"Don't sass me! Harbingers are non-violent. You lose your protection if you attack someone. It's not permanent. You get it back as soon as you stop attacking, but if you're stupid enough to get into a fight, then the magic won't protect you because it's an imbalance and magic is all about balance.

No one told you that you can't get involved, so I forgive you for putting your life on the line, but don't do it again. Fox can handle himself."

True, but before now I didn't know that I lose my magical protection if I fight, so it's not my fault no one explained the rules to me. I click once at her as I look Fox over, checking for more injuries than the bullet holes from Martin.

"Ok, good. Come visit me soon. Don't get yourself killed. Let Fox do his job. And if Santanos sends anyone else after Fox, that's basically the council green-lighting the fucker's death. You won't get a text from the depot about that one."

I click once more and then she ends the call with a quick goodbye. I hand Fox his phone back and look at the bodies just decorating the sidewalk like Halloween isn't five months away. Fox tends to leave corpses lying around, but I feel like maybe leaving these ones on the sidewalk is probably a bad idea.

Fox huffs an amused laugh and points up. "The cleaners follow me around. They take care of the bodies when I'm done with them."

I look up, but don't see anything out of the ordinary. Well, except the gargoyles watching over the alley—oh, wait. They're stone right now, but I bet my left nut they're not actually grotesques (never thought I would ever have an opportunity to use that architectural term). So, I wave at them, take Fox's hand, and pull him along to head back home, this time for sure.

CHAPTER NINE

*N*ext time for sure.

My dudes. I am tired. Can you please stop trying to get Fox to do shit he has zero intention of doing? And also, why the hell would this Santanos guy keep sending cannon fodder? Doesn't he have someone like Fox who might be able to give Fox a run for his money? Not that I *want* Fox actually hurt or killed. I'm just kind of surprised that bad guys really are stupid. Fox has literally killed like a hundred of Santanos' people, and the dude keeps sending groups of over-confident, under-competent goons to dull Fox's blade.

Maybe the blade really is dull because Fox gets fed up with it and starts shooting pretty quickly. These people are more of the pink mohawk gang, and their means of trying to detain my future husband was some kind of mesh. It looks like it hurts, but Fox isn't one to let a little smoking skin stop him from putting bullets into the heads and hearts of random attackers.

I wonder if I should let Annette know now that Santanos is dead as soon as Fox is ready to hunt him down, or if I should wait on that, because it seems like these two groups of pink-haired idiots were probably sent out as a single group and decided to split their chances.

I mean, it could be that Fox doesn't consider this a second attack and he'll wait for Santanos to send one more set of goons before carrying out his threat. It could also be that Fox is irritated as shit because we're half a block from home, hot showers, warm beds, and possibly all night snuggles.

He doesn't know that I am considering the possibility of a slumber party in his bed, but I'll figure out a way to tell him if I decide to sleep with him, even if I just make a show of crawling into his bed. I'd wait until he was pajama'd, of course. No sense in tempting myself too much before the third date. Gotta make sure we hit all the right steps before we get married.

I can almost hear the church bells already. I didn't know I wanted to get married in a church, but I can definitely hear the bells. Wait a fricken second. I really can *hear* the church bells. I glance at my phone, and it's not the top of the hour, so there shouldn't be church bells, but then as I'm looking for the source, I see a couple more gargoyles just hanging out on the low stone wall in front of the brownstones in this neighborhood. It takes me a second to realize that the sound is coming from them, and then it takes me less time than that to realize that they are conversing.

How awesome is that?

I wander over to them, listening to their chatter with a huge smile on my face while my soon-to-be beloved man finishes fighting the pink-mohawk gang down the sidewalk from us. The gargoyles don't stop their conversation on my account, and since I have no idea what they're saying, I appreciate just listening. Church bells have a pretty sound, but the language of the gargoyles is beautiful. Of course, just because it's beautiful to listen to doesn't mean they're not talking about dicks or something. I mean, I'd probably talk about dicks if I could talk.

"Romily."

A shudder of arousal knocks through me at the sound of my name on Fox's lips. I turn toward him, standing in the middle of another massacre, and find myself desperate for our third date. Damn, why do I have to have standards?

It's definitely cuddle time. I pat both gargoyles on the back and make my way over to Fox, grabbing his hand and running full speed toward his home. I don't want another interruption before we get behind the wards, and somehow we manage to make it inside his beautiful home before anyone else tries to attack. Bloody boots stay in the entryway, and I push Fox to the master bedroom so he can shower, then I take stock of my suit in the mirror in the hall bathroom. It's a bloody mess from transfer from Fox. I'll have to replace it, but spending that kind of money on a new suit will teach me to keep my hands off Fox after he's been working; I'm nothing if not tight-fisted and frugal with my own money. Some might call me *beggarly*.

Look it up, it's a synonym for being a Scrooge. Yes, I like puns. Get with the program; I'm like the ultimate dad joke waiting to happen.

Ok, off with the suit, into the shower.

I scrub up quickly even though I want to luxuriate because: hot shower. Drying off, I wrap my towel around my hips and head back to my room, leaving my bloody clothes for later. I dig in the duffel bag of my stuff from the apartment and slip into a pair of threadbare flannel pajamas and an oversized T-shirt. Whoever got my stuff was thorough; they even grabbed my frozen leftovers and the plants, which are sitting on the tables in my room—no, I don't feel bad about stealing Elijah's plants; he just left them to die.

I'll eventually replace my charity clothes with things I'll buy for myself, but not until I've worn them through. No sense in wasting money on lounge wear when my uniform is a suit that I have to wear from the time I wake up until I'm ready for bed. Being on call requires a certain amount of preparedness, which includes staying dressed all day long.

Once I'm decent, I scamper over to Fox's room and enter without knocking, delighted when I barge in on Fox in his birthday suit sewing up the holes in his torso. I give him a lascivious grin, deliberately letting my eyes travel over all that deliciousness. I would have probably even made it to his feet if my gaze hadn't gotten caught on his cock.

Not for that reason, you perv. Well, not *only* for that reason. I mean, it's a gorgeous cock, long and thick and just about right as far as I can tell, but that's not what stops me from taking in the all-of-him. No, my attention snags on the fact that my man is castrated. No balls. No hint of a sack. Nothing at all. What. The actual. Fuck?

I'm not saying that people don't do cruel things for no purpose—I'm mute because a douchenugget decided he didn't want to listen to a sick baby scream—but who castrates someone else?! Unless he had testicular cancer, and then it makes sense he wouldn't have balls, but they don't amputate sacks too, do they? Aren't there fake testicles? You know, the same kind of thing as when women get implants after having mastectomies.

On the plus side, even though he doesn't have balls, his dick works just fine, which I knew before because I could feel his erection, but now I get the pleasure of watching his cock go from flaccid to erect, and oh my, what a sight it is.

My dick responds in kind, as it should when I'm complimented so thoroughly, and it takes all my significant effort not to reach for him. Instead, I force my eyes to finish looking at the rest of him and force my feet to walk in a circle around him so I can enjoy the view from every angle, and then I take my happy ass to his bed and crawl under his blankets, watching him as he watches me.

For several long seconds we stare into each other's eyes, then Fox blows out a breath, looks away, and finishes sewing himself up. The wounds from the subway car attack have all but disappeared, leaving scars, but nothing so hideous that it takes away from his sexiness. Actually, looking him over and knowing what I know now about his lifestyle, I'm surprised he doesn't have more scars. The tattoos hide some of them, I'm sure, but seriously, he's been shot three times in three days and has gotten a lot of cuts from knives and swords; he has a lot of scars, but not nearly as many as I would expect.

Damn, my life is just full of mysteries waiting for me to unravel them. Fox and I are going to have some fun conversations soon. I can't wait to find out what happened to his balls and why his skin smokes when touched by chicken wire, *and also* why there's no evidence of burns now. I didn't see any damage, but I did see the smoke and I've never known smoke to exist without at least a little burn. Of course, we're talking about magic, so the rules of general physics probably don't apply.

After stapling closed a cut running from the top of his thigh to his hip, Fox pulls some sweatpants on (sans underwear), turns off the lights, and crawls into bed, facing me. I motion for him to turn over and when he does, I make him my little spoon, wrapping one arm around his chest and sliding the other beneath his pillow. He's taller than me, but that just means I get the pleasure of sinking into his warm scent with my nose pressed to the back of his neck. Sighing happily, I squeeze him briefly and let sleep take me into dreams of love and laughter and Fox.

CHAPTER TEN

The double chime of our phones wakes us up before the sun. Fox doesn't seem to have the disorientation of waking up mid-cycle that I do and rouses me with a shake as he puts my phone in my hand.

Squinting at the message from the depot, I have to ask myself whether they're cruel for waking me up two hours before my appointment time or if they're smart enough to realize it would take me an hour before I'd be ready to leave the house.

Instead of immediately getting up, I glomp onto Fox and pull him back down into a cuddle, laying over him and nuzzling into his chest. I float in a doze for a short while before Fox pats my butt and kisses the top of my head. "Coffee, work, breakfast date," he murmurs.

The words have the effect he intended, exciting me enough to roll off him and shoot him a happy smile as I head to my room, morning wood leading the way. He gives me a definitively heated look and palms his own erection, watching me walk away. We're going to have amazing chemistry as soon as I get him naked *after* our *third* date. This is me sticking to the plan.

Even though it hasn't been cleaned yet, I put on the brown and gold suit again. It complements my coloring and makes me feel sexy, and since we're going on a date after he kills a man, I want to feel like I look my best.

Putting on my makeup and fixing my hair takes less time today, because practice makes perfect, and in less time than I expect, I'm sipping on another delicious cup of fancy coffee, watching Fox strap on his weapons. He forgoes the sword today, sheathing a shorter, but no less deadly, blade. It's a bit over a foot long and shiny with a black handle wrapped in leather.

My timer runs down while he's getting ready, so I finish my last few swallows, give him a kiss goodbye, and put my bloody boots on, heading out the door. I should probably get the boots cleaned or figure out how to clean them myself. Leaving a trail of dried flecks of blood everywhere I walk is probably not the best idea.

A cab sits in front of the house, and the cabbie waves me over. As I get into the back, he turns and gives me a tight smile. I recognize his emerald eyes from the church run and the one after that. "Address?"

I show him the address on my phone and watch him input it into his GPS before he pulls into the flow of traffic. I wonder why Harbingers ride for free and why Fox doesn't ride with me? It would make sense to share a cab since we're leaving from and heading to the same place. He doesn't need that much extra time to get ready; we should discuss this, so I send him a text.

Me: *Is there a reason we can't take the same cab next time?*

Future Husband (I take great delight in knowing that he's getting messages from me with the same label): *Yes.*

Me: *Is this a reason I can intuit on my own, or are you planning to elaborate?*

Future Husband: *If I take a cab, I pay for myself. If you take a cab, you ride for free. But if I take you in a cab, I pay for both of us.*

And I like having the extra time after you leave to rub one out.

Me: **shocked gasp* *eggplant* *peach* *water drops* THIRD DATE.*

I don't use emojis; I write all that out with a silent laugh bubbling out of me.

Future Husband: *Some of us aren't that patient.*

Me: *I've been saving my next orgasm for you, and you're over there rubbing one out every chance you get. I should've known you wouldn't wait for me.*

Future Husband sends me a dick pic with his hand covered in cum.

Me: *Cheater!*

Future Husband: *You're the one with a plan. I'm just along for the ride.*

Wait just a gosh darn second. Fox doesn't have balls.

Me: *Where did that cum come from?*
Future Husband: *My dick?*
Me: *YOU DON'T HAVE BALLS!!!*
Future Husband: *I do.*

"We're here," the cabbie interrupts.

I check the time and sigh, putting my phone away and getting out, patting his shoulder in thanks. Clearly Fox isn't one hundred percent human, so now I have to figure out what he is, and I can't think of any mythical creatures that keep their testicles somewhere other than right below their dicks.

Maybe I'll google it while I wait for Fox to finish working.

The address is a duplex, and I'm supposed to go to the B apartment. I'm not sure if I should knock, but it seems rude to just walk into someone's home. Not that that's ever stopped me before. And really, the guy is going to die, so rudeness seems like a pointless worry. Eh, I'll split the difference.

I knock while turning the unlocked door—who keeps their door unlocked in this city? Anyone could waltz in off the street.

Like me.

I waltz into the house, startling the grubby man lounging on the sofa in a beer-stained white A-shirt and valentines boxers. A cigarette hangs from his lips and an overflowing ashtray sits at his elbow.

He looks at me, and I look at him, and then I sort of just step out of the way of the door, making sure not to touch anything. This place is dirty, and I don't say that lightly. I've been homeless; I'd prefer that to living here. And the man gives me the creeps.

"What's a Harbinger doing in Montenegro's pleasure palace?" His slimy voice oozes out of him as he grabs his junk.

Gross.

"Montenegro hasn't done anything to warrant a visit from a Harbinger, unless the Harbinger comes for the pleasure of his company."

He eyes me up and down, and if I wasn't one hundred percent sure he couldn't touch me, I might've walked out again. Slimy bastard. I don't know what he did or if he's Montenegro, but the guy is giving me the vibes and those vibes are saying he probably shouldn't be allowed to live on the same planet as me or anyone else.

Fortunately, before he can do more than creep me out, Fox shows up. He takes one look at me, unholsters a gun, and shoots the dude right between the eyes. It makes a bloody mess of bone and brain matter on the back of the sofa, but I feel better knowing he doesn't exist in this world anymore. Without a word, Fox unsheathes his really long knife and heads up the stairs. A few bumps on the ceiling above me later, a head comes rolling down the stairs, stopping at the bottom of the landing.

Huh. I guess Montenegro was upstairs.

Fox comes down after the head, leading four dirty children. My eyes grow wide at the sight of them; two kids between eight and ten hold onto two babies about the same age. It's a very Lemony Snicket visual for half a second, but the kids don't look at all sad at finding the two men dead, and their wicked smiles ruin the Snicket vibe.

Fox ushers us all out of the house before stopping to make a phone call. "Got them all alive."

He puts his phone back into his pocket and looks down at the kids. "Your parents will be here shortly. Stay with the gargoyles."

The eldest child nods. "Thanks for the assist."

Fox nods once, takes my hand, and leads me to the sidewalk. "They're older than you. It was a kidnapping and ransom," he explains. At my skeptical disbelief he adds, "The babies were born thirty years ago. It takes hundreds of years for cherubs to grow up."

Oookaaay. I would never have guessed that on my own. Good thing I'm not taking points away for wrong guesses. I squeeze Fox's hand, letting him know I understand, and he walks me over a couple of blocks to a hole-in-the-wall diner much like the one where we met.

I tense as we enter, but no one attacks, and the hostess seats us in a booth, smiling at my Fox with hearts in her eyes. "What can I get you to drink, Mr. Fox?"

Oh, did you think I was speaking metaphorically when I mentioned the heart eyes? No, she's fangirling for sure, but her pupils are actually shaped like hearts too.

"Coffee and apple juice." The coffee better be for me.

"Right away, sir. Um, can I get your autograph?" She holds out her notepad and pen.

Fox stares at it like he has no idea what it's for and turns away from her, sending me a silent plea to save him.

I laugh and look up at the girl, shaking my head. No autographs.

She scowls at me for a brief second before realization hits and she shoves her pen and notebook at me. "Can I get your autograph?"

I shake my head, shaking with laughter, and push the notebook away.

Huffing, the girl walks away, stopping to talk to one of the servers before heading back to the hostess stand.

I slide my hand across the table, taking Fox's as I pull out my phone. Dates require conversation, right? Not the silent kind we usually have. Actual words.

So about this balls thing...

I smirk at him as he reads my message and am gifted with his amusement twinkling in his eyes.

He types his answer under my words.

Internal genitals are a feature of many species.

And now I have to decide if I'm willing to play the game or if I should ask outright. I narrow my eyes at him, considering all the clues so far. Sensitivity to metal on his skin, but not to bullets under it. He's faster than a human normally is, but not so fast it's out of the range of possibility for a human. At least not that I've seen. He does make good time on our work runs, especially if he's taking the time to masturbate first. Oh, I have a good question!

Why don't you have more scars?

"They disappear after about a month," he murmurs in response.

Interesting.

How old are you?

He gives me a sly look, but it disappears as our server brings our drinks. "Good morning, Mr. Fox. Harbinger. I'll have your food out shortly," she says by way of greeting and then leaves without taking our order.

Not that we got menus.

I arch a brow at Fox, who sips his apple juice. "Just wait."

Since he's not going to explain what we're eating, I tap my phone again, reminding him of my question.

He looks up at the ceiling, telling me he's doing math in his head—how adorable is it that he does that every time he has to calculate? Also, how old is he that he has to calculate his age???

"About thirty-six hundred years. I don't usually pay attention to more than the passing centuries now," he replies in his soft, deep tone. Somehow I doubt he gets loud very often.

So, I might have a guess, but if I get it right, it will only be one point because I can't possibly pin down his subspecies.

Fae?

"A quarter," he agrees, then points to his dark eyes and shows me the fire in them. "Another quarter."

Part Fae, part demon.

Human?

"Quarter," he smirks.

Oh gawd. One more species.

Hint?

"The wings on my back aren't tattoos."

Oh. Now that is interesting. His back has script on it, a foreign language in an arc over a couple of black wings that could be from any kind of bird. Between the wings is a shield with a sword behind it and below that a smoking revolver. Like I said, they are totally mob tattoos. Well, organized crime, anyway.

And yes, Daddy runs a criminal organization, even if we are the good guys.

Angel?

I mean, we did just save some cherubs, so I know the angelic exists; it's not a bad guess.

Fox shakes his head. "You'll never guess."

Challenge accepted.

Raven shifter?

He shakes his head again, hiding his amusement behind a sip of juice.

I will figure it out.

Fox clears the amusement away as our server brings over a tray of food. She sets a skillet in front of me with fried eggs over lots of sautéed vegetables and potatoes with salsa on the side, adds a plate of lemon curd crepes (that's what she tells me they are), and sets down a side of cut melon. She gives Fox a platter covered in gravy, announcing it's chicken fried steak and biscuits and gravy, and then she wanders off without asking about condiments. Not that I need any, and it looks like Fox is getting his recommended eight cups of gravy a day in one meal, so he probably doesn't need to add anything to his either.

I eye his platter, shaking my head at the insane amount of gravy on it.

Are you sure there's actual food under all that?

Fox chuckles, surprising me with the sound. "Eat your food, Romily. The Captain doesn't allow leftovers."

It's like he says things to purposely leave me with more questions than answers. Like, who is the Captain and why is he obsessed with leftovers?

CHAPTER ELEVEN

After breakfast, our first stop is the clothier to replace my ruined suit. He chastises me for getting blood on his clothes but gives me a replacement and tells Fox he'll send a courier for the one I ruined. Apparently there's enough magic around to get bloodstains out. Who knew?

I pay for both the new suit and the cleaning service to teach myself a lesson even though Fox offers to pay for both. I wave him off and present my hand to the cashier, who scans my chip and deducts several thousand dollars from my account. It hurts, but I doubt I will ever again rub up on Fox after a job.

Fox's eyes dance with humor as he watches me grimace at the cost of my mistake, but he makes up for it outside when he kisses my lips and caresses my cheek with his thumb. "I want to buy you a gift," he murmurs softly. "Second dates include a little shopping, and replacing your suit doesn't count."

I feel my face brighten as my smile grows brilliant. I nod, excited about what kind of gift my man wants to buy me, but secretly I'm hoping he's got good taste or the wherewithal to know he doesn't and the wisdom to let me pick my own. People say it's the thought that counts, but if you don't know what your person wants, you should think about letting them pick it themselves. That thought definitely counts.

Taking my expression as the consent it is, he walks me to the subway. The line takes us to a shopping district twenty minutes away, and when we get back to the surface, he takes me to a brightly lit jewelry boutique.

Soul. Mates.

Jewelry is the perfect gift for me.

Inside, the store manager greets us, coming around the counter to shake Fox's hand. "Hello, Mr. Fox. Greetings, Harbinger. What can I do for you today?"

"Diamonds. Cufflinks, pocket watch, tie pin, collar chain, pocket brooch, and engagement ring." Fox gives me a level look. "The ring is for later."

Of course it is; that does not stop me from jumping into his arms and kissing the ever-loving shit out of him. I love it when the important people get on board with my plans.

The manager doesn't even blink twice; he just starts leading us around the room, starting with the engagement rings, because he wants to make sure to match the rest of my diamonds with that one even though it's the last gift I'll get.

Proving that he knows me well enough to pick out my engagement ring, Fox points to the three biggest diamonds the manager brings out and then asks if he can get anything bigger. And he said humans didn't have fated mates.

Without missing a beat, the manager says, "I can custom order anything, sir."

Which is how we ended up custom ordering a huge-ass diamond engagement ring that will definitely dwarf my little finger when Fox asks me to marry him.

The rest of the jewelry the manager presents matches the cut of the diamond we ordered (don't ask me, I know nothing about diamonds). The cufflinks go straight on my cuffs, the diamond encrusted gold watch gets clipped into my vest pocket, the diamond wing brooch goes under my pocket square in my jacket, and the tie tack and collar chain are added last.

Honestly, if I didn't know that no one could attack me and steal my shit, I would be nervous about walking out of the jewelers wearing this much money on my body and carrying a matching silver set in a pretty bag. Fortunately, no one is getting my riches as long as I don't attack them and negate my protection magic.

Sorry, Fox, you're on your own if you get caught in another trap. I can't help; I have too many diamonds to protect now.

Fox huffs a laugh after reading my message and wraps his arm around my shoulder. "Protect the jewels; they're almost as valuable as me."

Pretty sure the receipt in the bag has the monetary value of my jewels printed on it and it doesn't say "priceless." And that is all the sap you are getting from me right now.

Fox hides his grin in my hair, kissing the side of my head, which makes me laugh. He likes to pretend he's stoic, but I make him feel all the things. I think the only reason he hides it is for his reputation, and I'm just fine with that. His reputation precedes him, much like his Harbinger.

Speaking of, our phones chime at the same time, and when I check it, it's not a message from the depot.

Daddy: *I FOUND YOUR WEDDING PLANNER.*

Me: *Contact info?*

Daddy: **contact card**

I open the contact to the name Furion Steelhorse, which tells me nothing about the species or gender of the person.

Me: *Why are they my wedding planner?*

Daddy: *You'll figure it out. Go to the address now. I know you just bought an engagement ring. It's all over the gossip rags already.*

Me: *There are gossip rags for organized crime?*

Daddy: *And paparazzi.*

Me: *Can we kill the paparazzi?*

Daddy: *They take their lives in their own hands any time they try to photograph a Reaper.*

Me: *Is Reaper a title or a species?*

Daddy: *Both.*

"I'm not a Reaper by species," Fox murmurs in my ear as he steers me toward the subway again.

I snap my fingers in a display of "Darn it!" and pocket my phone to look at his.

Satan: *Come to the house for dinner tonight. Bring your Harbinger.*

Fox: *No.*

Satan: *I didn't call, but I will if you force me to.*

Fox: *Thank you for the warning.*

Satan: *I'll send a car at seven.*

Fox: *We won't be home.*

Satan: *That has never mattered, has it?*

I take Fox's phone.

Me via Fox: *Why does Satan want to have dinner with us?*

Me via Fox: *This is Romily.*

Satan: *He put me under Satan in his contacts?*

Me via Fox: *What? No. Obviously not.*

Satan: *I'm sure my son would much prefer having dinner with Satan than his own parents, but the Duke of Hell has better things to do than entertain the fantasies of the young and brash. Tell Arlington to wear a suit.*

Me via Fox: *We're busy tonight.*

Satan: *I'm aware. See you tonight, Romily.*

I widen my eyes at Fox as I hand him back his phone and take mine out.

That person is terrifying.

"Try growing up with him."

I think I prefer the cult that thought it was fine to cut my vocal cords out.

Fox stops in his tracks and narrows his eyes at me. "No, my parents are preferable to that."

I give him a skeptical look, which makes him have to hide his laughter by kissing me. It's a smiling kiss, and I love the way our grins fit together.

"I suspect you're going to like them as much as you like Annette," he assures me, and since we both know I would be marrying that woman if she'd found me first, that's some high praise for his parents.

I guess I'll meet the parents tonight.

Do you even have a suit?

He arches a brow at me and dramatically rolls his eyes.

Proud of his exaggerated expression, I take that to mean he does own at least one suit.

CHAPTER TWELVE

*F*or lunch, I take Fox to my favorite food truck for two reasons. First, I genuinely like Lionel's food, and second, he needs to know I don't need a job anymore. We weren't able to go meet the wedding planner; we had to work another job that took us away from that plan, but Fox promised we will as soon as we can.

The customers standing in Lionel's line eye me like a mark, which ok, that's fair. I am wearing more money than any of them have seen in their lives, but I'm not about to let any of them get within arm's reach of me. It helps that my date is covered in weapons, but none of them seem to take the threat seriously.

Oh wait.

Are you glamoured?

"Yes," Fox whispers with a laugh. "Did you think I was walking around unaccosted because I'm handsome?"

Honestly, I thought it was because people are stupid and would rather think you're cosplaying than that you have the confidence to walk around the city with actual guns and ammo visible.

"You're not wrong about people," he admits softly.

If you're glamoured, why did I see your weapons at the diner and the library?

I assume that being his Harbinger gives me some immunity to the glamouring magic.

Fox gives me a curious look, giving a minute headshake. "Probably have a tiny bit of Fae in you. That's the only reason I can think of."

The only reason that doesn't piss me off is because I have passive magic now. What's the use of having ancient Fae ancestors if you don't get the benefit of power? I'm ok. I'm breathing and not being mad. It's fine. I'm fine.

When we reach the front of the line, Lionel looks me over with an arched brow, glancing at my companion and crossing his arms over his burly chest. "Two Manchkin Specials!" he hollers over his shoulder, then turns back to me, deadpan as you like, "I've been blinded by the bling because this cannot possibly be Romily Butcher standing before me as the Harbinger of Arlington Fox."

I give him my brightest smile, covering my surprise that he knows about the whole magic thing. Maybe that's how he got off the street. If so, good for him. Like I said, if I'd ever had a kernel of power, I would have used it to do right by me, so I don't blame him for doing the same if that's how he picked himself up.

"Still as annoying as ever. Money covers a multitude of sins, but no one likes a back-talker," Lionel teases as I slide him a five-dollar bill.

I push air through my lips, making a pfft sound, and jerk my thumb at Fox.

"Mr. Fox doesn't exactly count as a normal person," Lionel disagrees.

I grin up at my man and kiss his cheek affectionately.

"Huh. Yeah, this makes sense now. He's the only person with the personality and patience to put up with you," Lionel decides, looking between me and Fox.

Fox doesn't react at all to Lionel, treating him the same way he treats everyone else, and that's fine. Reputation to uphold and all that. I'm just glad Lionel approves. It would have hurt my heart if he hadn't, but I didn't know that until I brought Fox here.

"At least I don't have to employ you now. I wouldn't have paid you a fair wage and that might have given me stress-induced heartburn. Here's your sandwiches. Get out of the way. I don't have time to visit with you all day."

He slides our sandwiches through the window and pats my hand as I reach for them.

He's gruff and has a hard-ass reputation to uphold, but he likes me, otherwise he wouldn't give me the friends and family menu item.

I pass Fox his sandwich and wave to Lionel, happily walking off as I unwrap the goods. Who doesn't like bacon, cheesy eggs, and toast?

I lead Fox over to a bench and sit with him, watching the people pass as we eat. Most of these people are probably human, unaware of the magical man sitting right next to me. They're going about their lives like they always have, and a week ago, I would have been right there with them. It's crazy how a week can change a person's life.

Well, it's crazy how dramatically better *my* life has gotten in the last three days. I mean, I'm now sporting diamonds as part of my uniform. That's a Cinderella story if I ever heard one, right?

Do you think I'm Cinderella?

Fox reads my message and shakes his head, clearing his mouth before replying. "Flynn Ryder."

I think about that for a minute and shrug.

Ok, Rapunzel.

Fox chuckles, and the sound goes straight to my dick. Damn, he has a good chuckle. Rich, deep, full of the promise of joy if I ever get him to actually laugh. That's a bucket list item: hear Fox's unreserved laughter.

On the heels of his laugh, church bells start ringing all around us. We both look around for the gargoyles, and I spot fifteen at first glance. They've appeared in pairs all around us, mostly hanging out on the facades of the buildings, but two have appeared as statuary bookending the bench we're sitting on. I reach over and touch the stone gargoyle, petting it between its erect bat ears.

Fox leans over to the gargoyle next to me. "I didn't get a message from the depot."

The volume of the church bells increases all at once, then all but the gargoyle next to me go quiet. Fox listens to the gargoyle for a minute before standing, pulling me with him.

He hails a cab and puts me in it, rattling off an address to the cabbie and shutting me in with a quick parting kiss.

He turns back to the gargoyle and crouches down, petting the beast like I was as the cabbie takes me away. I wonder why we're taking separate vehicles this time?

It takes an hour to get to the right address, and when I arrive, it's another church. Knowing how awful the last one was, I step out, looking up to find the roof lined with silent gargoyles. Hundreds of them. A chill passes over me as I walk into the churchyard and up the steps, opening the heavy wooden door with a loud creak.

The inside of the church smells like burning candles, though none of the candles are lit. A stone of instinctual unease sits heavy in my stomach as I walk into the sanctuary, which is illuminated only by the sun filtered through the stained glass windows. As I step past the first row of pews, a black cloud of smoke appears and coalesces into the form of a black-skinned demon sporting horns and a mouth full of jagged, bloody teeth. In his hand hangs a mostly headless gargoyle, no longer stone, but recognizable nonetheless.

Blood drips onto the red carpet in front of the altar as the demon lifts the body and takes a bite out of it, staring at me the whole time. My steps falter at the crunch of bone and the tearing of raw tissue, but I straighten my spine, level my gaze, and finish the march to the front of the church.

The demon's laughter echoes through the empty sanctuary and hangs in the air like an oily substance. It halts my progress because it's just so eerie.

Tossing the body aside, the demon runs at me, faster than I can track. It bounces off my magical protection and goes flying across the room with the same force it hit my ward. Growling in anger, it gets to its feet and runs at me again, flying off at another angle when my magic prevails.

The demon charges and bounces off me over and over for ten minutes while I stand like a statue hoping it's not wearing down my defenses. It worries me that it's not flagging; Fox has competence in spades, but this one creature might be more than enough to seriously injure him. I don't know enough about his magical attributes to know if he's killable, but fear that he might not be indestructible pokes me in the vulnerable parts of my heart and mind.

I hear the front door open as the demon takes another header into one of the stone columns, and I turn to see Fox stalk inside holding the biggest blade I have ever seen. It's at least as long as he is tall with the flat of the blade stretching six inches wide. The upper half is smooth and sharp, gleaming like chrome, while the lower half is serrated with deadly teeth that drip a cloudy gray substance that dissipates as it leaves the blade. He holds the massive weapon in one hand and points the end of it at the demon in challenge. At least one of my fated mate's species must have super strength; Captain America has nothing on him.

Even though I'm twenty feet away from the demon, I know I'm in the way of this battle and back up, rounding the end of the pew opposite the demon to make my way to the back of the church. Fear for my Fox slithers into my heart, but I punch it down, choosing to believe in him rather than fear for him. Nothing in his stride, bearing, or entrance makes me think he isn't capable of handling this problem. He believes in himself, and so do I, dammit.

The demon gets to its feet, baring its teeth at Fox in some kind of facsimile of a smile. It's laughter oils the air again, then it changes. It grows bigger, bulkier, and armored. Spikes shoot out of its back, and a long sword appears in its hand, dripping the same ethereal smoke that falls from Fox's blade. Without pause or hesitation, my man attacks, moving forward faster than anything and striking the demon.

Their weapons clash, splattering the dark smoke around them so quickly that soon a fog surrounds them, obscuring my view of their battle. That might be a good thing, because to be honest, my nerves are unsettled. Fox is efficient and skillful. It never takes him long to kill everyone in his path, but the demon matches him swing for swing and doesn't look like he's flagging. I *know* Fox doesn't have an endless supply of energy; I've seen how he pants after a massacre.

I kind of want to throw up. I won't, because that might make Fox think I don't believe in him, but I kind of want to. Worry isn't an emotion I'm very familiar with. I don't like it. Fox better make it out of this battle whole, or we're going to have words about his life choices.

Alive and whole is better than badass and dead.

The loudest, most inhuman shriek I've ever heard fills the sanctuary, making my ears hurt with just how god awful it is, and the clashing of metal suddenly rings silent. The fog dissipates in a matter of moments, revealing the demon's head making the wailing noise about ten feet away from where its body stands frozen for a few seconds before it collapses to its knees, hunched over, but not toppled.

Fox wields his blade double handed and cuts the demon's body in half down the middle, getting stuck about a foot into it. He doesn't pull the sword free; instead, he starts sawing, using the serrated half to finish the job. Ichor, filth, and blood a shade of red so dark it looks nearly black spill out as the body loses its structural integrity and starts separating.

It's gross, and while I can handle a lot of gore, this is more than I want to watch, so I look away, pulling out my phone and taking a short video of my man at work and texting it to Annette.

Me: *I should get hazard pay for having seen any part of this.*

Daddy: *All of your pay is hazard pay.*

Me: *It's strange that no one bothered to tell me that.*

Daddy: *It's easier to hook the Harbingers in with loads of cash and promises of protection. No one wants to know that their entire paycheck is hazard pay.*

Me: *Speaking of hazards…Can my ward be worn down?*

Daddy: *Probably, but not by attacks. The ward gains power from each attack against you. I'm not sure what would wear the magic down, but magic is all about balance. Something out there can destroy your ward.*

Me: *That's worrisome.*

Daddy: *Don't ask me questions if you don't want honest answers. Are you going to visit Amos and Co. tonight?*

Me: *No. We're having dinner with "Satan" (not the Duke of Hell).*

Daddy: *That's what I said: Amos and Co.*

Me: *Then, yes.*

Daddy: *You're going to meet one of Fox's parents tonight. When you see him—you will know exactly who I'm talking about—tell him he looks like a Chris.*

Me: *Should I expect a positive or negative response?*

Daddy: *Both. If you send me a video, I'll buy you a bracelet to match your engagement ring.*

Me: *Done.*

Daddy: *God, I fucking love you.*

I slip my phone in my pocket and look up to watch the tail end of Fox dismembering the demon by cutting off the last chunk of its remaining leg. By chunk I mean the rest of its arms and legs are scattered in multiple pieces around the two halves of the torso. As soon as that last chunk comes off, the screaming cuts out.

It's a blessed relief for my ears when the church bells start up. Fox breathes a heavy sigh and hangs his head for just a second before standing up and limping—*limping*—toward me.

He's a bloody mess, and a gash on his temple along with the hand not dragging his sword behind him are both dripping a concerning amount of blood. I hold myself still, not sure about the protocol for an actually injured Fox, fisting my hands as I watch him make his way down the aisle.

"Romily." His soft utterance silences the cacophony of the gargoyles outside.

Right now would be a great time to be able to talk, but I can't, and I never learned how, so the best I can do is try to mimic the way a mouth forms words, which ends up with me clicking an approximate T-sound three times at him. *What do I do?*

"You're really bad at that," he chuffs, swaying a little on his feet.

I huff and take a step toward him, but he holds up his dripping hand. "No. Demon blood is poisonous. You wouldn't be able to touch me anyway. The gargoyles will get me home. Take a cab. I'll meet you there. I have to go through decontamination first, and that can take an hour if the poison is in my blood."

Fisting my hands at my sides, I project my frustration by scrunching up my face and huffing. I follow that up with a stern look and a finger point, then draw a heart on my chest and mime reaching out and throttling him Homer Simpson style.

Fox blinks at me, a little dazed with the level of my affection for him, and nods. "I'm really hard to kill, and every time someone does, it gets harder for the next person. I haven't died in almost a hundred years. It would take a demon much more powerful than a djinn to get close. Don't worry, your plans for a happily ever after are still safe."

There is a lot to unpack in that random supply of information, but now is not the time. I point to the front door and walk along with him, forced to stay about a foot away by my own protection ward, to the front of the church and out into the yard. A swarm of bat-like creatures—gargoyles in their flesh form—swoop down from the roof and disappear with my man as soon as we're outside.

CHAPTER THIRTEEN

A cab awaits me in front of the church, so I climb into it and give the man a wave in the direction of Fox's home.

"Home, Harbinger?" the man asks in an accent so genteel, I know that this guy is *not* a cabbie.

So, I get the fuck out of the car and start running. I do not have time for an abduction today.

I hear the door of the cab slam and footsteps following me, catching up, of course. It's not like he can attack me, and hopefully my ward believes that abduction is a kind of attack. It would suck if the guy was able to get his hands on me and relocate my body without my explicit permission.

Church bells ring out in front of me just as a gargoyle appears on the sidewalk, wing extended as if pointing the way for me. I'm not dumb enough to get confused, and I follow the direction of the pointing wing, pivoting to cross the street without so much as a glance to see if it's safe. I trust my gargoyle friend.

Friends.

The next one turns me in the middle of the road, sending me into the middle of an intersection while horns blare behind me. The next gargoyle sends me crosswise across the intersection to the soundtrack of a screech and a crunch of metal and glass. I don't turn around, I don't slow down, I jog with purpose, following my gargoyle friends as they lead me through the city and keep me out of the hands of my would-be abductor, or whatever he is.

Breathless and tired, I finally make it to the brownstone, collapsing against the front door before I turn to see if my pursuer managed to follow me. A line of gargoyles sits on the low wall demarking the edge of Fox's property, and on the other side, a man with more freckles than a red-headed step child breathes heavily as he looks at me with laughter in his pale purple eyes. "I'll catch you next time, Harbinger," he says before giving me a salute and jogging away. Before he gets too far, he calls over his shoulder, "Tell Fox, Santanos won't be attacking him again."

Great. Fox set a boundary, everyone agreed to his terms, and he forgot to include me in it.

I walk into the house, typing out a message to my future husband.

Me: *Santanos has agreed to your terms. He swears he won't attack you or send anyone to attack you.*

I don't immediately get a reply, so I pocket my phone and crouch to unlace my combat boots, jumping out of my skin and crab walking backwards when the front door hits me in the ass. I only stop when I see Fox giving me his worry-eyes as he pushes the door closed behind him. I guess running home took more time than I thought.

"Did Santanos do something?" he asks, bending to help me get my shoes off.

Aww. What a sweet man.

After the gargoyles absconded with you without so much as blowing me a kiss goodbye, the cabbie waiting for me at the curb turned out to be a bit too upper class to be a real cab driver, so I booked it out of the car and started jogging home. Our lovely church bell singing friends guided me through the city causing who knows how many fender benders, but I got home without a scratch on me. You might have noticed the line of gargoyles on our wall? Anyway, the person chasing was nice-ish. Just told me to let you know that Santanos won't attack you again. Oh, and he might have threatened to "Catch me later."

Fox stills at the last part, rereading it twice before he very carefully pulls my boots off and sets them aside. Fury rolls off him in hot waves that are not just a descriptive technique and press against my skin. His anger is palpable and beats against my body for several minutes while he grips my ankles and stares a hole into the wall somewhere behind me.

I sit still, pinned in place by his emotional outburst and waiting for his anger to cool or for him to give me a clue what I should do. I knew the man liked me, obviously; he bought me diamonds for fuck's sake. I didn't realize the depth of his affection. The almost suffocating fury on my behalf is more than anything he's ever put out on his own behalf. It makes me feel *cherished* and also wonder which part of his heritage he gets this empathic ability from.

"Next time, let him catch you. It will give me permission to kill Santanos," he murmurs, squeezing my ankle and rising.

He offers me a hand and pulls me to my feet and into his arms, hugging me as he buries his nose in the crook of my neck. Yes, of course he changed clothes; I'm not ruining another suit and my ward wouldn't let me near him if he was still covered in demon ick.

I run my hands up and down his back, stunned by both his words and his emotional display. He *wants* me to let myself get abducted? Isn't that counterintuitive to keeping me safe? Not that my ward will let me get hurt unless Santanos knows how to negate it. Somewhere out there, something exists that can make my protective magic null.

I shudder at the thought, reminding myself that if Annette doesn't know what it is, Santanos likely doesn't either.

"You'll be safe, Romily, and I'll get to kill the annoying cockroach."

I pull back from his hug, typing fast before showing him my phone.

Getting abducted doesn't make me feel safe, but I'll do it for you because you really want to kill a guy and because you're so good at it. Competence is sexy, and I just can't bring myself to withhold from myself the gift of watching you eviscerate a man. Or whatever he is.

"He's a hybrid plus like Annette. The plus is whatever gifts the council has deigned to give them, and no one except the council knows everything about those gifts."

Look at you, explaining things no one asked you to explain. I'm proud of you for using your words.

Deadpan as anything, "I have to make up for the words you refuse to use."

I widen my eyes and drop my jaw, exaggerating shock and offense on behalf of my disability.

Fox snorts and pushes my mouth closed, then melts me by pressing his lips to mine. The kiss starts soft and affectionate, just the press of lips, the quiet comfort of connecting with the person who gets you. My Fox gets me. He understands my words, especially the unspoken ones, the ones that matter the most. His tongue darts out, and I open for him, giving him the access he wants, the taste we both crave. Our tongues slide together, tangle up, and dance, eliciting a delightful groan from my man that vibrates against my lips and causes them to tingle. I press my body flush to his, gratified when his hands grip my ass, kneading the soft flesh there as he pulls me as close as two people can get with their clothes on.

It's almost enough to tempt me to amend my three date plan, especially because I'm meeting the parents tonight. Almost.

Before my horniness can actually change my mind, I pull back from the kiss, pecking him a couple times and stepping back so I can't rub my dick against his. I smile up at him, projecting the affection I have for him as I type a few blind words into my phone.

I really like you.

Autocorrect must be on the ball today: no mistakes!

He huffs and squeezes my butt again. "Me too."

I giggle and pull him to the couch so I can cuddle him. We need a few hours of nothing to do.

CHAPTER FOURTEEN

"The house" Satan, aka Amos and Co., invited us to for dinner isn't a house; it's a goddamn mansion. *Sprawling* is the way I would describe this ridiculousness. So many square feet I could get lost in it and have to break a window to escape. Oh, and it doesn't actually exist in the city. We took a tunnel, one that I have traveled through on many occasions, and instead of coming out on the other side where the tunnel always spits everyone out, we exited onto a country road lined with trees overhanging it like a romantic Hallmark movie. At the end of the road, there was the mansion, spread out in the late afternoon light. We left the brownstone at seven and arrived at the mansion at two in the afternoon (my phone updated my time zone, so that puts us in the UK or some parts of Africa—I'm guessing UK).

It's been a disorienting experience, and we've only just arrived.

The butler lets us into the house, greeting Fox with a forty-five degree bow executed with the kind of deference that makes me wonder if my boyfriend (yes, I think we're ready for labels) is a prince. I mean, he's not related to the Duke of Hell, but he's almost all mystery, and the wealth on display here makes me wonder things.

The butler leads us to a parlor decorated with rich reds and Victorian brocade patterns. Sitting on the sofas are three men with drinks in hand who stand as soon as we walk in, interrupting their chattering conversation.

"Son!" A man with long pale blue hair and shiny grey eyes floats over to us with a happy smile, widening his arms for a hug. He has delicate features in both face and body, but he's taller than Fox. I can see where Fox gets his lithe form; some might call his father willowy, but I see he's compact rather than soft, just like his son.

Fox reluctantly wraps his arms around his father. "Athair."

The man steps back and pats Fox's cheek with a grimace. "I can't believe you showed up with this scruff on your face. It's shameful for a Fae to have body hair."

One of the other men pulls Athair away from Fox. He has the same dark hair Fox has and a pointed chin strap beard. He's wider than either Fox or his athair, but it's uncanny how much Fox and this man's hands are alike. Strong with veins standing out—oh, and the forearm veins! Clearly Fox is biologically related to him too.

"Hello, son," he says with a wicked smirk. "Don't listen to your father, he's just jealous you got my dashing good looks."

"Pater," Fox sighs, hugging the second man and shooting me a long-suffering side glance. "Where's Omp?"

Pater waves toward the sky. "Communing with the moon or something. He said he would be back in time for dinner."

The third man looks like the love child of Thor and Captain America with mid length wavy blond hair and the bluest eyes I've ever seen. He has a strong jaw and cleft chin, but the rest of his features are a bit softer in that boy-next-door way. His biceps are bigger than the other fathers and his tree trunk legs make me think that at least one of the other two probably climb him regularly. He's shorter than both of the other fathers, maybe a little above average, though shorter than Fox. I have to bite my tongue to wait for introductions, because this is clearly the man Annette told me about, but I slip my hand into Fox's pocket and retrieve his phone as I ready mine to take a video. I'm getting my diamond bracelet, dammit.

"Father," Fox greets his third parent, who kisses his cheek and claps him on the back before all three men turn to me. I start the video and grin brightly at the three men.

"This is my Romily Butcher. These are my fathers, Tag, Amos, and Bear." He introduces them in the order they greeted him, the Fae first, then the demon, then the Chris. "My other father will join us later."

I shake each man's hand in turn and show all three my phone, while pointing it toward Bear—I wouldn't want anyone to be upset about a secret video, so I make sure they all know they're being recorded.

You look like a Chris.

Tag and Amos erupt in laughter as Bear narrows his eyes, gritting his teeth. "I'm going to shave that red hair and pluck all her eyelashes and wax her brows off." He points a thick digit at my phone. "I will have my revenge, woman!"

Laughing, I end the video and wrap my arms around the poor man, hugging it out so that he doesn't hate me, though clearly he's already placed the blame on the right person.

He squishes me in a hug, quietly laughing in my ear, "If you ever tell her, I'll deny it to my dying breath, but I did consider that name for my next identity. I love the Marvel movies."

I give him an assuring squeeze and pat his back to let him know his secret is safe with me. Unless Annette bribes me with more jewelry, then all bets are off, but he doesn't need to know that.

Stepping back, the other two fathers take their turns hugging me, welcoming me into their family.

Tag brushes his long, Smurf-blue hair off his shoulder, smiling warmly at me after our initial hug. "How did you get Arlington to agree to marriage? We've been trying to get him settled down for two thousand years. He's ridiculously stubborn about his freedom."

I shoot Fox a smirk and a wink before typing out my response.

It was totally his own idea. I'm just along for the ride. I have no idea why he would ever want to decorate me in diamonds.

I blink my most innocent, unbelievably naive expression at them all, causing Fox to huff, pulling me into his side, kissing my temple.

"We're not engaged yet," he mumbles.

Tag squeals, jumping up and down, clapping his hands. He grabs both of Fox's other fathers by their arms and shakes them. "Did you hear our boy? He said *yet!* I am going to get to plan a wedding after all!"

I shake my head and pull up the message from Annette and show it to him:

Daddy: *I FOUND YOUR WEDDING PLANNER.*

Tag scowls at the phone. "Who is 'Daddy' and why do they get to pick your wedding planner?"

I make a show of sending the video of Bear's reaction to "Daddy" and wink at them.

After a minute, Annette's reply comes through.

Daddy: *Fuck, that's funny. Let me know the cut of your ring.*

Me: *Ask Fox. I don't know anything about cuts.*

Daddy: *God, you're just a pretty face, aren't you?*

Me: *This is why I need a sugar daddy.*

Daddy: *Good thing Fox found you.*

"Oh my godlings, you are just like her," Bear gasps, reading our conversation over my shoulder. "Amos! There are *TWO OF THEM!*" he bellows with trepidation.

Amos takes my phone, reading the conversation before handing it back. "Arlington, are you marrying both of them?" he demands seriously.

Fox makes a gagging noise, stepping back and dragging me away from his pater. "Fuck no!"

Oh. My. God.

Fox just raised his voice.

Holy shit.

I wish I'd gotten that on video. That's amazing.

I stare up at my boyfriend in shock and awe, slowly lifting my phone and starting to record just in case he does it again. Actually…

I steal his phone again and type out my demands.

Do that again, just like that so I have video evidence.

Fox reads my message, takes his phone, and hits the stop button on my recording. He glares at all three of his fathers before walking over to the bar and pouring himself a golden-brown drink from a crystal decanter. He swallows it all down in one shot, refills his tumbler, and turns back toward us to silently brood.

Man, I had no idea brooding Fox would be just as sexy as murdery Fox. He's such a temptation.

JENNIFER CODY

Sighing because I really don't need to pop wood in front of Fox's fathers, I turn back to them, typing out my question.

Did all of you donate to create Fox or what?

What? Mpreg is a thing in some of the books I read. If I can have a magic ward keeping me basically indestructible, males can have babies. That's all I'm saying.

Tag rubs Amos' belly affectionately. "Yes, we did, and Amos carried our son for almost a full century, but of course our boy was a bit eager to get into the world. He came three full years early. Scared the shit out of all of us, but he was a strong baby."

Amos kisses Tag's hair. "He'd just cooked long enough, he wasn't premature."

I widen my eyes at Fox, conveying in no uncertain terms that no one is going to be pregnant for a century, especially not me.

Fox gives me a flat look and subtly shakes his head, agreeing with me that we'll adopt when the time comes. At least that's how I'm interpreting that look, and no one is going to convince me otherwise.

The butler returns then, announcing dinner, and we all make the shuffle to a formal dining room where a massive giant of a man occupies the space at the head of the table. He has hair the color of thunder clouds that stands on end in a puff like he rubbed his head on a balloon. Dark blue eyes study us impassively as we enter but soften when they fall on me. He meets me at the table, pulling the chair to the right of him for me.

"Hello, Harbinger. Thank you for joining us for dinner. I'm Dakota, Arlington's omp," he greets me, shaking my hand and shocking me with the static electricity coming off him. "Apologies, it takes a while for the energy to rebalance after a storm."

I give him an enthusiastic smile, trying to figure out what the hell he means, but honestly, I don't want anyone to just tell me. I really want to figure it out for myself. This is the mystery quarter of my man, and he thinks I can't guess it.

I sit in the chair Dakota assigned me, with Fox on my right while Dakota sits at the head and the rest of his fathers take up the chairs to Dakota's left across from us. As soon as we're seated, a couple of servers bring the first course of this dinner, setting small amuse-bouche plates in front of everyone. No one has the same thing on their plates, but everything looks delicious. I'm a little jealous of what Fox gets, though I'm greedy enough not to want to share mine to taste his.

Do you think the chef has leftovers we can take home, so I don't miss out on what everyone else has?

I set my phone between me and Fox as I tip the first bite onto my tongue.

The corner of Fox's mouth lifts for a second before he dips his chin once.

And that's the extent of our conversation because then Tag takes over, worming his way into my heart and my wedding plans. I haven't even met my wedding planner yet, but I already know he's going to have his hands full with my future father-in-law.

CHAPTER FIFTEEN

Nooooo! This is not the way to wake me up every morning. Especially when I get home after midnight and then the depot sends me to a den of iniquity before I can even get my shoes off. It was a nursing home, by the way, and Fox killed a non-literal angel of death—you know, the serial killer kind. Now everyone's forgotten relatives won't die at the hands of their nurse.

Ok, I am a little cynical about nursing home facilities, not because of the staff, but because of the little shits who put their parents in a home and then never visit them. I might have volunteered at a couple of facilities because volunteer work is a good way to get a free meal.

Damn, I'm bitchy this morning.

The text from the depot informs me I have an hour and a half to get across the city, so I get my crabby ass out of the warm bed and into a hot shower. When I get out, a steaming cup of creamy coffee sits on the counter, waiting for me, and I swear that's the moment I fall in actual love with Arlington Fox.

Coffee is apparently the way to this man's heart, so clearly the old adage is true. I'll have to see if it's also true for Fox, but since he eats without appreciating the taste of his food, it might be hard to convince his stomach to let me squirrel into his heart. I'm up for the challenge, though; no way am

I giving up a man who knows how important my coffee is. Especially now that I've discovered fancy coffee comes in multiple flavors. Toasted almond should be on everyone's coffee wish-list.

As soon as I'm dressed and decked out, I head to the front room, where Fox ambushes me with hot, needful kisses before I even see him. He groans as our tongues meet and greet each other and pulls me into his erection. This is almost better than coffee, but he's going to owe me another cuppa.

Arousal flushes through me as he thrusts his hard-on against mine, nearly convincing me to forget that we have work to do, but the timer on my phone going off reminds me that there are people to kill. With a growl of annoyance, Fox steps back from me, holding me at arm's length.

Feel free to send me another dick pic.

I wink at him as his dark eyes heat with predatory arousal. He reaches down as he stares at me and adjusts his cock in the yoga pants he's wearing. Ok, I can see why he might want to rub one out before going into public.

"Third date today," Fox informs me as I back up to my shoes.

I nod an enthusiastic agreement, then get my boots on and head out to the cab awaiting me. The driver is the same one that I've had a couple times now, and since he's becoming a familiar face, I lean between the seats to read his name on his ID: Belaphor Betelgeuse.

Nice. That's a name to remember.

I show him the address from the depot and sit back, pulling up my book because I'm not in the mood to talk to anyone. At least not until I get a dick pic from my boyfriend.

Ungh. His cock is delectable. I'm so going to get it in my mouth tonight. And so help the depot if they interrupt…oh. Hmmm. I wonder if that will work?

Me: *I am getting laid tonight, so if anyone needs to die, they'll have to wait for Fox until tomorrow or die by someone else's hand.*

Depot: *What time?*

Me: *Starting at 8 PM.*

Depot: *Until?*

Me: *8 AM?*

Depot: *Noted. Twelve hour sexcation confirmed.*

Huh. It worked. I totally got us off the clock for twelve full hours! Go me!

Fox: *Did you tell the depot we're taking a sexcation?*

Me: *Yup!*

Fox: *…*

Fox: *Good call.*

Me: **grin* *peach* *eggplant* *waterdrops* *drool**

Fox: *Emojis exist.*

Me: *But this way you know I've intentionally sexted you.*

Fox: *Valid.*

Confirmed: I adore this man. I love that he validates my wonderfulness. Who could possibly resist this kind of unconditional support? Not me; I'm not even trying. I'm going to have to tell him I love him someday. Maybe when he gives me my big ass diamond ring. That's the right occasion to tell someone you love them, right?

I pull my book back up and dive back into the nerd-jock ridiculousness. FYI, jock did in fact have a gay freakout. It was as funny as I thought it would be. I'm now at the eighty-percent break-up. You know what I'm talking about: the characters break up for a couple chapters because of some stupid miscommunication. These two are doing the overheard-something-out-of-context break-up trope. It's fun. I mean, I'm no expert on healthy relationships or anything, but it feels like if you break up once over something this stupid, you're not likely to end up with an actual happily ever after, right? I have zero experience in this arena, but I hear that marriage is even harder than dating, and if you're breaking up while dating…well, I'm not going to assume these guys are going to make it to the whole until death do us part thing. Just saying, this is their first long term relationship, probably not their last.

I would never let Fox break up with me over something stupid. I mean, it's not like he's ever going to overhear me talking about anything out of context. Snicker. Benefits of being mute.

"We're here. Do you want me to wait?" Belaphor asks as he pulls to a stop in front of an alley.

I glance at the address on my phone and back to the alley, noting that the GPS on the dash says we're exactly where we're supposed to be. I pat

Belaphor's shoulder to thank him and nod. I wouldn't mind not being surprised by another potentially kidnapping cabbie.

Stepping out of the cab, I look at the addresses on either side of the alley and then sigh, walking down the damp corridor until I reach a well-hidden stairwell that leads to the basement of the building on the right. The numbers on the wall match the address, so I descend into the dim stairwell and walk through the loud, creaky metal door at the bottom.

I enter an empty hall lit by flickering fluorescent lights. Four doors evenly spaced along the walls tell me nothing about what I'm supposed to do here. The hall ends at a T with more of the same emptiness broken by unmarked doorways. I can't announce Fox's imminent arrival if there's no one to see me, but no one gave me any instructions.

Turning, I study the halls and doors, wondering if I should just start knocking, but I dismiss that thought when it clicks in my head that the little black domes in the ceiling between the fluorescent lights are cameras. I look up at the one above my head and smile up at it, waving my fingers. That's a good enough announcement of my presence. The rest is up to Fox.

I lean up against the wall at the end of T, keeping my ears open for any noise from any of the three halls around me. Well, I suppose it's two halls that intersect, but geometry was never my thing, so it's three halls.

This is boring. I pull my phone back out and start reading again. I'm almost done with this book anyway.

I get all of two and a half sentences read before one of the doors down the hall in front of me opens and a head peeks out close to the floor. Curly black hair styled in a fluffy afro surrounds the most cherubic little face I've ever seen in my life. Big brown eyes stare at me in surprise, then another angel face with shiny floofs of puffball pigtails pops out of the door above the first face. This one has the prettiest hazel eyes and a smile so full of joy it literally brightens the corridor with its brilliance.

The children exchange a smiley glance and then dart out of the doorway, running straight to me and crashing into my legs as Fox walks out of the same doorway, short knifey sword in hand and dripping with blood. I guess he took a different route into the building.

I put my phone in my pocket and crouch down, grabbing both toddlers and standing with them, kissing each of their cheeks before looking back at Fox with a question on my face.

He rolls his eyes, exaggerating the movement. "They're older than you," he reminds me before breaking the knob off the next door and kicking it in.

A screech sounds, but it's cut off fairly quickly after Fox disappears.

I look down at the cherubs in my arms, smiling my amusement at Fox's insistence that I remember these cuties are older than me. They giggle with me, scrunching up just like toddlers do when they laugh, then Fox emerges from that door with two more cherubs in tow. Since this looks like a cherub rescue mission, I sit on the floor and pull all the babies to me.

Fox looks between me and the four baby cherubs and points at the baby with the pigtails. "She has two doctorates."

My jaw drops, and I look down at the toddler in my arms. Her delightful smile turns decidedly mischievous. "I still a baby," she assures me in toddler speak.

I look up at Fox again and point at the girl.

He shakes his head. "Two. PhDs," he emphasizes.

The girl sticks her tongue out at him and blows a raspberry. "Baby PhDs!"

One of the other cherubs whispers in my ear, "She's still a baby. She's a baby with doctorates. Our parents encourage us to fully explore our interests. She likes school."

This one looks about two years old but talks to me like a dry professor or boring doctor. Wow. I don't even know what I would say if I could speak, so I just hug the babies to me and pretend they aren't older and more educated than me.

Fox decides to leave me to my own devices and proceeds to continue the rescue mission, opening door after door until the puppy pile of cherubs surrounding me is sixteen strong. He disappears at the end of the hall to my left for a while, and when he returns half the babies are asleep, and the other half are running along behind him. That's right, all sixteen of my cherubs decided it was naptime, and he brought sixteen more with him from wherever he disappeared to.

I frown at the thirty-two cherubs in the corridor and send Fox a text message.

Me: *I am bothered by how many cherubs we're rescuing today. How did this many kids go missing before you were called?*

Fox mustn't like the answer because he texts me rather than speaks.

Future Husband: *That is a very good question. Cherubs are used for their brains; every one of these kids is a genius. It's hard to believe that 1. No one reported any of them missing before all of them were missing, and 2. None of them were clever enough to escape on their own.*

Me: *The cherubs from the other day were being held hostage by only two men, why didn't they escape?*

Future Husband: *They were in magical manacles; they were weakened by the magic, which for cherubs means they were rendered stupid.*

Me: *The manacles are magically spelled to make whoever wears them weak, and for cherubs, their brains are their strength, so the manacles make them stupid. Did I interpret that correctly?*

Future Husband: *Yes.*

Me: *So ask one of the cuties why they're still here and why no one reported them missing.*

Fox's lips turn down for just a flash of a second before he turns to the cherub clinging to his pant leg. "Why didn't you escape before I got here?"

The cherub looks up with huge, watery eyes. "Gorgons scary."

"How long have you been here?"

The cherub shrugs. "Long time."

Me: *Gorgons as in turn-you-to-stone?*

Future Husband: *Yes.*

"They took us from boarding school in the fall," a little voice chimes in from behind Fox.

They'd been missing for months? It's already close to summer. What the hell?

Me: *Is it our job to investigate this?*

Fox: *No.*

I arch a skeptical brow at him.

Fox: *But it may behoove us to follow up.*

That's what I thought.

Me: *Is anyone coming for these babies?*

Fox: *At least seventy years older than you.*

Me: *You baked for a hundred years before you were born. I think age is just a number at this point, don't you?*

Fox: *Yes. A bus is coming to take them to the processing center where their parents will be able to pick them up.*

Me: *Parents who didn't report them missing?*

Fox: *We'll follow through.*

The door creaks open and Annette walks in, power red stilettos clicking on the tile, followed by a cadre of uniformed people wearing cargo pants and long sleeve t-shirts. Annette stops outside the puppy pile, angry face studying the toddlers around me and behind Fox.

"This is unacceptable." She snaps her fingers to a man standing on her left and behind her. "*Jameson!* Find the headmaster. I want an accounting. Interview all the teachers, parents, everyone you can. I want to know why no one reported these cherubs missing. Which one of you sent the SOS?" she questions the kids, all of whom awakened at the first bark of her angry-voice.

My two-PhDs tot raises her hand. "Me, Miss Killian."

I turn wide eyes onto my favorite little cherub. No one reported her missing? She had to orchestrate her own rescue and it took her *months* to do it?

White-hot anger rises in my chest for these kids. I don't care how old they are, they should never have been abducted and certainly not forgotten or deliberately hidden.

Annette picks the cherub up and hugs her. "Good job, baby. I *will* make sure you are all protected. None of you will be leaving my care until we figure out how you were taken without anyone reporting you missing." She turns her furious gaze on me and Fox. "Heads *will* roll for this offense."

Fox dips his chin once as I nod vehemently; whoever took these kids will rue the day they got on Fox's radar. Annette will make sure of it, and I'll be right there to witness the fruits of their regret.

CHAPTER SIXTEEN

It was optimistic of me to believe that the depot would give us time to actually go on a date before our sexcation. Immediately after the cherubs were on the bus taking them to the processing center, my phone chimed with the next location. I knew going in that Fox didn't get many days off, but when my phone chimes a fourth time, I suspect that someone is playing with me.

So far Fox has annihilated the people keeping the cherubs, some random homeless guy—no idea what his crime was—and a group of dickheads in a board meeting. I'm not saying the dickheads didn't deserve to die, but a vacuum of power in any large company probably isn't good. Even if the people dying are evil.

Not my problem, though.

My problem now is the building in front of me. It looks like a warehouse on the outside, but it's one of those warehouse-turned-club things that crop up every now and again. I've heard of this place. The owner is one of those rich philanthropists nobody actually trusts, but he funds some of the resources that the homeless in this city rely on. I don't actually want him to be the target, because that might be bad for the people I know. It would have been bad for me a week ago.

Just in case, I check the address, but unfortunately I'm in the right place,

JENNIFER CODY

so I put some steel in my spine and enter through the front door. I pass the entry way and the cash desk and come to a full stop when my feet pass the threshold to the main floor, agog at the sight that greets me. It's…it's an orgy. I can't even emphasize that enough.

Ok, let me set this scene. In front of me is three steps down into a large pit/dance floor with a disco ball hanging at the dead center. To the left and right of the dance floor and three steps up are rectangular platforms with comfortable, overstuffed couches and tables. Directly across from me is another three steps and a smaller platform with a throne dead center, and behind it another three steps up, a platform with, uh, interesting furnishings that include lots of ropes and padded benches.

Groups ranging from two to seven people occupy the lounge areas and the furthest platform, engaging in sex acts that would make me blush if I didn't have a vivid imagination and a backlist of raunchy books I've read and loved. Under the disco ball, a naked man kneels, tied up in white rope with his arms crossed over his chest and his legs splayed to show off an angry red cock that someone tied up in a fancy bow.

It's important to note that the warehouse lights are on, lighting up the entire space without leaving any shadows to hide anything going on. Absolutely nothing is left to the imagination, and I think that's a damn shame. There's something to be said for dim lighting when everyone's naked. Sex is fun, but it's not the most glorious thing to watch unless you're viewing porn, and that's a production, not—whatever the hell is going on here.

The tied-up man at the center of the pit glares at me through angry, bloodshot, blue eyes and shouts around a bright red ball gag. He's not the owner of the club, but he is one of the people in the background of photos of the owner guy—a bodyguard or something; I don't pay enough attention to know.

On the throne across from me sits a blond guy who looks like he's not old enough to be in the club, but as we've all learned in the last week, the body doesn't always reflect a person's age. After all, Fox looks like he's about thirty.

The guy on the throne is naked, of course, petting the blond curls of a man on his knees worshiping his cock. Behind the guy on his right side stands a giant, vaguely Asian, naked guy with his arms crossed, scowling at me while his comically large dick juts out next to the young guy's face. The young guy has one leg tossed over the arm of his throne to make room for the guy bobbing on his dick, and he holds the other guy's cock in his free hand, absently playing with it as he watches the guy in his lap.

"Hello, Harbinger," the guy on the throne says without looking up. His voice doesn't rise above the noise of the people fucking all around the room so much as it absorbs the noise, muting them while he speaks, but as soon as he stops, the noises continue at full volume.

He gives a laconic wave toward the tied-up guy. "I've prepared the sacrifice." He looks up and black eyes meet mine as a wave of pure lust washes over me and sinks into my bones. The lust isn't directed at anyone in the room; it's pure, physical, urgent arousal.

I step back, wide eyed, trembling with the effort to not reach for my cock, stumbling when I hit a warm body behind me. Arms come around me to help stabilize me, but they tighten instead of releasing me as soon as I find my balance.

"Gotcha," a cool, genteel voice whispers in my ear, full of amusement.

Oh shit.

"The ward doesn't protect you from harmless magic wielded without malice towards you. And I have no malice toward you," the dude on the throne says.

I take a deep breath and sigh, and then try to get my visceral reaction to the lust thrumming through my veins back under control. My eyes might roll up when the guy behind me shifts just enough that his hard cock nudges my butt cheek. I'm not even attracted to him, but the sex magic in this place makes me desperate for another person to touch me.

Ugh. Fox needs to get here before my higher thinking skills are completely paralyzed.

With more effort than it really should take, I lift my hand and present my middle finger to the man I'm assuming is Santanos. I've never known a better way of silently communicating "fuck you" than flipping people the bird. It also works as a "fuck off" and a "go fuck yourself." It's a versatile gesture.

Santanos laughs, muting the noises around us again, though no one actually stops fucking to pay attention to us. "I'd heard you were the silent type. Perfect for Fox. I wonder if you'll break your silence when you orgasm."

Another wave of his magic hits me hard. Arousal more potent than anything I've ever felt spins in and around me. Resistance is hard—pun intended—and fuck if surrender isn't easier. Santanos' magic is pure temptation. Even as I give in to the need, I know I'll be pissed later. I let the magic pull an orgasm out of me, leaving me breathless and raw, spinning in a whirlpool of all-consuming lust.

"Interesting," Santanos grunts, audibly annoyed.

The whirlpool drowns me in Santanos' magic. The lust isn't satiated by the orgasm, and though my logical mind doesn't believe it will help, I let myself surrender to it again. Weakness and fatigue roll through me; the only thing keeping me on my feet are the arms of the man holding me up. I rest my head on my captor's shoulder, too tired to resist and too fuzzy for anger. The anger will come later, but right now, I just want to sleep.

No. I can't sleep yet. I will, but not before Fox gets here. Where is he?

"Wakey wakey, eggs and bakey," the man holding me up murmurs, jostling me enough to rouse me.

I slowly lift my head, discovering that I must've passed out for at least a few minutes because I've somehow gone from across the room to standing before Santanos.

I blink at him, bringing my brain back online after it's mini vacation. I still feel weak and raw, but fury slowly heats in my gut, giving me the energy boost I need. I'm not ready to shake off the guy holding me up yet, but I will be.

Santanos looks at me like an interesting bug, like he might actually want to stomp on me. "I marvel at your silence, Harbinger," he announces with enough sarcasm that I feel like I can safely assume he's mocking me.

Or not.

Another wave of his magic rolls over me, and the next thing I'm aware of is the tap of someone's hand against my cheek, pulling me back to consciousness.

I crack my eyes open, greeted by the face of the guy who chased me through the streets yesterday. He…looks concerned.

I'm not humble enough that I don't know exactly how good I am at reading people. Body language is my thing. I'm good at projecting, and I'm good at reading. So when I stare into the purple eyes of the man looking down at me and there's a moment of connection and understanding between us, I know that he's going to do something to help me. And somehow I just know it's going to be soooooo stooopid. Seriously. He's about to go against his boss, and even I know Santanos isn't a dude to mess with.

The guy—I desperately need to know his name so I can stop calling him "the guy" or "the would-be abductor" or other inconvenient things—helps me stand back up, grabbing the lapels of my suit to pull me back to vertical.

He turns me back toward Santanos, who's looking rather annoyed at this point.

"I have brought warlords to their knees and sent them crawling home to cry in their mother's laps," Santanos growls, leaning forward on his throne three steps up from me. "Everyone screams for me."

I blink at him, somehow unsurprised to discover he's a narcissist who can't be bothered to think things through when he doesn't get his way. Surprise, surprise. Santanos doesn't know I'm mute and hasn't seen past his annoyance to figure it out.

Where the fuck is Fox?

I'd probably save myself some dick torture by informing Santanos of my disability, but because I'm an antagonistic brat sometimes, I only find the energy to smirk at him. I'm sure I have some reserves somewhere, but this bastard has basically ensured that I won't be able to get it up tonight when I'm supposed to be sexing it up with my boyfriend.

Who's finally shown up.

I feel the atmosphere in the room change when he steps into it. Santanos flicks his eyes behind me and leans back in his throne again. "Fox. You've finally come to see me."

The guy holding me moves us to the side at a gesture from Santanos. When he gets us turned around, I shoot Fox a glare that says, "What took you so long?"

Fox studies me from the top of the steps across the room, impassively eyeing my disheveled state and the wet spot on the front of my trousers. The blank mask he always wears while working slips just enough for me to get a peek at his fury, but as he flicks his eyes back to Santanos, the mask slides back into place.

Fox descends the steps, exuding confidence with every step as he approaches the bound man at the center of the dance floor. He unholsters a gun and holds it pointing down until he brushes by the bound man. The gunshot is deafening in the wide-open space of the warehouse. My ears ring as the body goes limp, unable to fall to the floor because of the tension from the ropes binding it.

Santanos' voice covers the silence after the gunshot, which is the only reason I notice that the orgy going on around us has stopped. I'd kinda just tuned it out as background noise until now. "Now that you've fulfilled your misguided duty, let's talk."

Fox's stride never falters as he walks right up to me and pulls me out of the arms of *the guy*. His focus centers on me as he cups my jaw and looks into my eyes. He doesn't speak, but he doesn't need to. His eyes ask me if I'm ok, they project his sincere worry for me, and they tell me that he loves me.

Dammit, right now is not the time for this mush! I flatten my lips, roll my eyes, and then press a quick peck to Fox's lips. Tapping his gun hand, I turn him to face Santanos. That's the best way I know to tell him to kill the fucker on the throne.

"*Seriously?!*" Santanos exclaims. "I've had him for a full fifteen minutes and you can't even be bothered to ask him if he's ok? No wonder your Harbingers keep quitting. This is why you need to come work for me. You're evil minion material to the core."

That's what this has been about? Santanos is trying to recruit him? What the heck? I thought he wanted him dead?

Fox lifts the gun and shoots him. Just like that. Of course, the bullet stops about an inch from Santanos' face and drops on top of the head of the guy in his lap. Oh yeah, I forgot about that dude. I don't know how because he hasn't stopped blowing Santanos the entire time, but ya know, I've been distracted.

Santanos smirks at Fox. "The council doesn't want me dead."

Dammit.

Fox empties his gun. It's a waste of bullets, and even though my ears are ringing, it's kind of satisfying that Fox doesn't have to say a word to tell him to go fuck himself. Reaching back, Fox takes my hand and turns away from Santanos' smug grin.

I grab the man behind me by his shirt, tugging him along as I follow Fox. He was going to rescue me; I feel like I should return the favor.

"You can't have Bellamy," Santanos calls, which makes the man in my grasp stumble to a halt.

Fox and I both turn back toward the throne. I glance between Santanos and the man in my grip, Bellamy—yay for having names—and pull him away from Santanos.

Fox gives me a questioning look, but the answer is right on my face: Bellamy is mine now. He nods once, grabs Bellamy and pulls him behind us. "My Harbinger has claimed him."

Santanos scowls at Fox. "He did not."

Fox tips his head slightly. "Romily, are you claiming Bellamy?"

I grin at Santanos, showing him my teeth, and nod.

"You can't have my assassin!" Santanos roars, furious and seething with power.

I feel his magic hit me, but this time it washes harmlessly over me. I guess he's feeling a bit attacky now. Ha!

Grabbing Bellamy again, I turn my back on the seething man and march us out the front door, unhindered and free from attack.

And now I have my very own assassin. Ok. Now I have another assassin, but I don't think Fox would consider himself one. I don't know. He's a Reaper; that's not quite the same thing.

CHAPTER SEVENTEEN

My cab waited for me, so I push Bellamy into it and crawl into the middle seat with Fox joining me on the other side.

"Home," Fox tells Belaphor, who's stuck with me all day.

Bellamy leans forward to look at both of us. "Why?" he questions, genuinely confused.

Fox doesn't respond, so I pull out my phone and try to reason out a response for him.

First, I didn't know I could just "claim" you. Second, because fuck Santanos.

Bellamy reads that, gives me a weird look, and a panicked laugh bubbles out of him. "Really? You just decided taking me would be a good 'fuck you' to Santanos?"

I excel at nonverbal communication.

"Santanos doesn't like it when people take his toys away. You're going to get one or all of us killed," Bellamy informs me, regaining his composure and speaking in the same posh tone that he usually uses.

"You're the only one in any danger," Fox murmurs, sliding his hand onto my knee and squeezing it to reassure me.

"Because I'm the only human in this car."

I'm human.

Bellamy pffts at my message. "You were before you became a Harbinger.

Now you're an immortal human plus. I'm just a human. I don't have magic protecting me."

I turn to Fox, exaggerating my surprise on my face and he nods.

"The magic of a Harbinger makes you immortal. You would continue aging and dying if you ever decided to quit," he explains.

Isn't it lovely how I've already trained Fox to be more communicative? I'm a goddamn miracle worker, aren't I? Mute boy trains the silent type to talk in less than a week. Amazing.

Fox gives me a bored look, almost like he knows what I'm thinking.

I grin at him and kiss his cheek, turning back to Bellamy, who appears to be studying me.

"You're mute."

It's not a question, but the surprise is clear in his tone. It's like the depot announced who I am and sent everyone pictures but failed to tell them I can't speak. Actually, that sounds like something Annette would do just because it's funnier when everyone assumes I can actually talk and just choose not to.

Don't worry, Fox and I will protect you.

I spin back to Fox, typing out a question that needs answering.

What exactly does it mean when a Harbinger claims someone?

"I don't know," Fox replies softly. "It's something Harbingers can do, but I don't think anyone ever has."

The information flow toward new Harbingers really needs to be revamped and streamlined.

Me: *So. I claimed someone.*

Daddy: *Who?*

I turn to Bellamy and take his picture, sending it along.

Me: *Bellamy. I don't know his last name.*

"Jones," Bellamy says, unashamedly reading over my shoulder. "Who's your daddy?"

"He's talking to Annette."

Daddy: *Good choice! I bet Santanos is pissed! *three laughing emojis**

Me: *Yep! He needs to die.*

Daddy: *Someday. Hopefully. But it's pointless because he'll just be replaced.*

Me: *Ugh. The balance of magic is as dumb as me.*

Daddy: *You're not allowed to say that.*

Me: *I didn't *say* anything.*

Daddy: *Does Fox know about your obsession with puns?*

Me: *Fox loves my puns!*

"No one loves puns," Bellamy mutters.

I scowl at him.

Go read a Xanth novel, you cretin. Puns are hilarious.

Me: *How do I unclaim someone who hates puns and reads private messages over my shoulder?*

Daddy: *Already? But you just got him!*

Me: *I'm just not sure he's worth keeping at this point. Also, what does it mean that I've claimed him? Fox doesn't know.*

Daddy: *I'll have to ask the council, but you can always talk to Dakota. He's a council member.*

Me: *Ooh. Yes. I will message him. I'm still trying to figure out his species. DO NOT TELL ME. Fox thinks I can't figure it out.*

Daddy: *I hate to agree with him, but I kind of do.*

Me: *I'm going to show all of you how good my Google fu is.*

Daddy: *I'd never bet against you, but I might start a board for how long it takes.*

Me: *Put me down for a week.*

Daddy: *Done.*

Fox disappears from my side, alerting me that we've made it home. I climb out after him while Bellamy gets out on his side.

It's well past eight, so I know I won't be getting any more texts from the depot, but I'm still more than a little pissed about what they did today. And Santanos. My balls hurt and I'm too exhausted to be bothered to go out again. Plus there's the whole thing with Bellamy coming home with us.

As soon as I get my boots off and change out of my dirty clothes, I head to the fridge, pulling out the containers of leftovers that we got last night. My stomach thinks eating itself is a good idea, but I convince it that food is a better option by shoving some of the cold amuse-bouches into my pie hole.

Fox joins me, opening another container, while Bellamy stands awkwardly eyeing all the ridiculous number of tables everywhere.

I agree with his face when it questions the sanity of someone who collects tables, but I scowl and shake my head when he opens his mouth to comment.

He quickly changes what he was going to say. "Is there enough for me?"

Without a word, Fox holds out a container to him.

We have seven containers, so we do have enough to share, but as soon as Bellamy opens it, I steal a couple of the bites from it. I brought them home so I could try them; I'm not missing out because we have an unexpected guest.

Bellamy side-eyes me but wisely chooses not to comment.

I think I'm hangry, which is weird for me because I'm used to not eating all the time and I've never been grumpy about it.

As soon as the initial gnaw of hunger abates, I make grabby hands at Fox, and he hands me his phone after bringing up his father's message thread. Damn, this man is easy to train.

Proud of him for reading me correctly, I kiss his cheek.

Me: *This is Romily. How are you, Omp?*

McQueen: *I am well. What can I do for you?*

Me: *Well, what are my options here? Are you all powerful, and I can ask for anything, or is this limited to reasonable requests?*

McQueen: *I'm not omnipotent, and I reserve the right to refuse service to anyone.*

Me: *Fair. But I get special consideration because I'll be your son-in-law soon, right?*

McQueen: *Sure.*

Me: *Your answer has earned you the privilege of walking me down the aisle.*

McQueen: *I'm honored.*

Me: *I claimed someone.*

McQueen: *Send the details to Annette.*

Me: *I did, but no one knows what it means for a Harbinger to claim someone, so I'd appreciate some clarification from the council.*

McQueen: *I'll send Annette the details so you can read them for yourself, but the takeaway is that you've basically adopted him. Congratulations.*

Me: *I'm too young to be a father!*

McQueen: *Too late. No take backs. I'm a grandfather now.*

Me: *I'm going through a tunnel. You're breaking up. Krrk. Oh darn. I've lost the connection.*

McQueen: **laughing emoji**

I hand Fox back his phone and point at him accusingly.

Fox takes my hand and kisses the back of it as he hands Bellamy his phone so he can read what Dakota said.

"At least you don't have to raise this one," Fox murmurs, pulling me in for a hug.

I consider that and shake my head. I do actually have to raise this one. He needs to learn to appreciate puns or he's no kid of mine.

"Ridiculous. I'm at least fifteen years older than you," Bellamy announces, handing Fox's phone back.

Age is just a number, kiddo.

Bellamy reads my message and turns a fun shade of pink. "No."

It's too late. You read what Grandpa Omp said, no take backs.

"You're not even married," Bellamy argues.

Best to just start off on the right foot. You have four grandfathers now: Grandpa Omp, Grandpa Athair, Grandpa Pater, and Grandpa Chris.

Fox flashes me a smile as Bellamy reads that.

"I'm going home," Bellamy decides, turning toward the front door.

I grab him before he gets three steps, smack his butt, and point my finger at him, shaking my head, then point to the floor in front of us.

Fox interprets for me. "You live here now, son."

Fox makes it so easy to love him.

"I am not living in a house where the dining tables outnumber the actual number of residents," Bellamy argues, deadpan.

"Please have Bellamy Jones's residence packed up and move his belongings to my home. Sell all the furniture except the tables." I didn't even see Fox pick up his phone, but I can hear a quick response from whoever he called.

"No!" Bellamy protests, but it's too late. Fox has already hung up, a smug look on his face.

"We'll find a place for your tables," he assures our boy.

Bellamy scowls at us both. "I *liked* my bed."

Your new bed is amazing to sleep on.

I pat his chest to reassure him.

"You can't just take me from my home." His arguments are getting weaker. I sense capitulation around the corner.

How about an ice cream?

Bellamy pouts as his shoulders droop and he nods. "This is ridiculous."

I guide him over to the table in the breakfast nook and sit him down, patting his back before grabbing a carton of mint chocolate chip from the freezer and three spoons. Fox brings the bowls and scoops out our dessert, and in silent agreement he and I sit on either side of Bellamy, making sure he knows he can't escape—I mean, that he's welcome into our new little family.

"I'm not calling you 'Dad.'"

"Don't be ridiculous," Fox murmurs. "Call me 'Oppa.'"

Obviously I'm Papa.

Fox nods approvingly as Bellamy looks at him with an expression of utter disbelief. "Your reputation is a bald-faced *lie*."

Fox taps the rim of Bellamy's bowl. "Finish your ice cream. It's past your bedtime."

"Please send me back to Santanos."

CHAPTER EIGHTEEN

I'm startled out of a dead sleep by the sounds of both phones going off. I roll over to check mine, but Fox's arm pulls me back as soon I have it in hand, making me his little spoon. I pull up the text from the depot and it takes me a long few seconds for my sleepy brain to comprehend the words.

Messengers of Evil (I renamed them yesterday): *Paternity leave approved. Confirmed two days leave. Congratulations on your new addition!*

As soon as I understand the message, I drop my phone on the bed and snuggle closer to Fox. I assume he did this.

My phone almost immediately chimes again.

Daddy: *Why am I getting a notice of paternity leave from HR?*

Me: *We adopted Bellamy last night. Obviously we need some time to adjust to parenthood.*

Daddy: *I'm too young for grand sugar babies.*

Me: *It's too late. No take backs. You're a grand sugar daddy now.*

Daddy: *Imma buy my boys matching father-son outfits.*

Me: *I approve. Make sure his says "mini me" on it.*

Daddy: **evil smiling emoji**

A bang on our bedroom door almost makes me regret claiming the thirty-five-year-old punk on the other side of it. "Why am I getting a notice from the depot that I'm on *naternity* leave for two days? I don't even work for the depot!" Bellamy calls through the door.

I pick up my phone and text him.

Me: *1. You realize that I can't call back through the door, right? 2. Did you just say 'naternity'? 3. New parents take leave all the time. We just want to make sure you get settled in before we have to go back to work. You were a surprise! We don't even have a sitter lined up.*

Bellamy sends me a screenshot of the depot's message to him, which does in fact call his leave "naternity."

Our First Child: **middle finger* Make sure the sitter is hot or I will run away.*

Me: *Done.*

Our First Child: *I'm going to make sure the moving company doesn't break my shit.*

Me: *Bring jelly donuts.*

"And bear claws," Fox murmurs sleepily.

Me: *And bear claws.*

Our First Child: *I'm not sure I'm old enough to buy donuts on my own.*

Me: *If I have to buy them you're eating Grapenuts for breakfast for a month.*

Our First Child: **middle finger**

I let my phone fall back to the bed and sigh when Fox kisses my neck, hugging me a little tighter. We didn't do anything but crawl into bed last night. I was too tired both physically and emotionally. When I wrapped him up in my arms and spooned him from behind, the entire ordeal with Santanos finally caught up with me, and I just had to cry it out. Fox let my tears soak into his T-shirt and didn't say a word.

It was nice, and I feel fine this morning. I've been through worse things than a few forced orgasms, but obviously this was far more personal than attempted murder.

For a while, I soak up the warmth of being in Fox's arms, dozing in and out of wakefulness without truly falling back to sleep. After a time, he kisses my neck again and pulls away, taking himself to the bathroom, which makes me aware of my own pressing needs.

When he doesn't emerge after five minutes, I roll out of bed and head to the hall bathroom, taking care of my morning ablutions there. I haven't moved my toothbrush and other bathroom products out of here yet, so I put that on my mental agenda for today.

The only thing I did last night before falling into bed was move my clothes out of Bellamy's room. Fortunately, today can be a lounge day since we have the time off, so I don't bother changing out of my threadbare pajamas before heading to the kitchen to make coffee.

Bellamy sits at the table in the breakfast nook with a box of donuts in front of him and a steaming mug of coffee in one hand. As I pour myself a cup from the coffee pot, I have to admit that fatherhood suits me; I already have my kid trained to provide caffeine and donuts. I'm amazing.

Bellamy follows my movement with his violet eyes as I sit across from him and pull out a donut from the box. His face, perfectly fine when he went to bed, now sports a darkening bruise on his left cheek. I point to it, arching a brow in question.

Bellamy sighs a bit dramatically. "Santanos doesn't like having his toys taken away," he repeats. "There are minions posted to encourage me to go back to him."

Ok, look, I know Santanos sending people to beat up my kid is serious, and I shouldn't laugh, but not even the threat of Armageddon could have stopped the silent laughter that bubbles up at his words. I know people who have actual minions. *Minions!!!* Who has minions in real life? No one, that's who. Except Santanos. Wait.

Me: *Do you have minions?*

Daddy: *Thousands of them. Why?*

Me: *Just...making sure this is my life now. I'm your favorite minion, right?*

Daddy: *Eh. It's a toss-up. Depends on how much I like my grand sugar baby.*

I snap a photo of Bellamy and send it to her.

Me: *Put his photo on your wall. He needs to see his new family has accepted him.*

Daddy: *I'll frame it and everything.*

And my life used to be boring.

"I'd forgotten what it was like to be ignored by my parents," Bellamy deadpans, picking up another donut.

I'm not ignoring you. I'm reporting your assault to the authorities. Like the wonderful Papa I am.

Bellamy scoffs. "You know, I was Santanos' favorite assassin for a reason."

Like father, like son, I suppose. I guess I should invest my new fortune in first aid supplies. You and Fox are going to send me to the poor house just keeping you in bandages.

While Bellamy reads that, my phone chimes with a new message that he unabashedly checks instead of giving me my phone back. He taps my screen a few times and then his phone chimes.

"Why am I in your phone as 'Our First Child?'"

I take my phone back to see what he's done, discovering a file sent from Annette that he's forwarded to himself. It's the information on a Harbinger's claim. The breakfast nook quiets as we both start reading.

Eventually Fox comes in, planting a kiss on my head as he joins us for breakfast. He starts reading over my shoulder but interrupts himself with a tap on the table.

I quickly forward him the file and continue reading.

Dakota's takeaway from the information is actually a fair summary, but there's some extras he didn't mention. The way the document reads, it seems like Harbingers are held in special regard by the balance of powers, but the information about *why* that is just isn't there. Harbingers and the Avatars (Annette and Santanos) are the only other people afforded the ward of protection that I have, which kind of explains the bullets that stopped midair yesterday. Kind of because I bet if I was shot, the bullet would ricochet or bounce back or something like what happened to the demon.

Why Harbingers are given the same protections as the Avatars isn't explained, although the file does tell me that I can extend my protective ward to Bellamy, if he agrees to submit to my claim. He won't be limited to non-violence like me, since my non-violence is a prerequisite for being a Harbinger, but his would be limited to defensive violence only.

Basically, I adopt him, provide for his needs, and protect him, and Bellamy is allowed to function as a bodyguard for me and back up for Fox. It's like taking a job that includes room and board and then your employer suddenly decides you're family forever and ever and never lets you quit.

I suppose that's why Harbingers haven't claimed people before me; it's quite the commitment. Eternity is a long time. Not that I expect to be a Harbinger forever, but I will be as long as Fox needs me.

How long have you been a Reaper?

My question makes Fox pause, staring up at the ceiling. I hide my laughter behind a sip of coffee, waiting for him to finish calculating. "About fifteen hundred years."

"What?" Bellamy asks, looking up from his reading.

"How long I've been a Reaper."

Bellamy nods, impressed and curious. "No one really gossips about you."

Fox's dry look could mummify the living. "There's nothing to gossip about."

"Well, except for that one story that everyone likes to repeat," Bellamy continues without even acknowledging Fox's assertion.

I perk up at that and tap the table, clearly communicating the need for him to tell me the story.

Bellamy blinks at me and I watch the process of his decision-making cross his face. He's not sure if it will be more satisfying to pretend he doesn't know what I want or gossip about Fox with him sitting right there. I admit, it would be a tough decision for me too.

Of course, Bellamy splits the difference. "Want something, Papa?"

Pride at how quickly my boy's growing up splits my face into a grin. Then I none too gently pat his face, conveying my insistence he tells me the story.

Bellamy winces against the sting of my pats. "Abuse," he whines.

I tap the table insistently.

"Fine," he grouses. "I have no idea how accurate this is. It is the only story I've ever heard about Fox, and it happened when his name was Timothy Blackblade of Avon."

I gasp, widening my eyes and turning to Fox.

He blinks up at me from his reading. "I change my name when it's appropriate."

I narrow a scowl at him accusingly.

Your parents call you Arlington. What's your real name?

"We call each other the names we've chosen. My original name was Macfilsenghe," Fox explains, and I can hear the exasperation in his voice but don't understand it until he explains. "They bickered for a hundred years about what to call me and gave up when I was born and just named me 'son.' My real name is Arlington Fox until I age out of it."

And just because it's adorable to watch him calculate, I ask, *How long have you been Fox?*

As predicted, he looks up at the ceiling as he thinks and returns with, "Fifty-two years."

So he'll be Fox for another thirty or so years. It'll be interesting when we have to change names. I'm bad with remembering the year. Sometimes it takes me until the fall to stop using the previous year. It's going to take ages to switch from calling him Fox.

I turn back to Bellamy and roll my hand for him to continue.

"So, back when he was Blackblade, a large coven of vampires descended on Paris. They were killing people indiscriminately and turning fledglings by the dozens. Fox was in England at the time, so the powers that be sent him to end the massacre in Paris. He entered the den, facing down a thousand feral vampires. No one knows exactly what happened that night, but when the sun rose in the morning, the only evidence that the coven ever existed were the bloodstains on his clothes and the bite marks on his body."

Fox huffs. "The story has been exaggerated. I got to Paris three days after the original coven arrived and there were only a few hundred vampires in the city. It took me another three days to hunt them down. And I left the Parisian vampires alone."

"Since then, everyone knows not to interfere when Fox is on the hunt. It's why the people he targets don't bother running. They know they don't stand a chance of escape." Bellamy eyes Fox with respect I didn't realize he had for my man. "You're the reason I got recruited to Santanos' side."

Fox assesses Bellamy, looking for the rest of that truth in his lavender eyes. "Why?"

"He thinks if he can make me as immortal as you, I'll be a match for you." Bellamy levels his gaze at Fox, sitting back. "He's wrong."

Fox grunts at that. "If you accept Romily's claim, he won't be."

"If I accept the Harbinger's claim, there will never be a test of skill between us," Bellamy corrects.

Because the person a Harbinger claims is called an Acolyte, and they exist to stand with a Reaper, defending the Reaper's back.

"I would spar with you."

Bellamy hums softly and flicks his gaze to me. "I'm going to accept even if you're the most ridiculous person I've ever met."

I grin at him, flattered that he likes me.

We'll be a family until Oppa retires from reaping.

"Why are you so embarrassing?" Bellamy whines.

"Don't talk to your Papa that way," Fox says, pulling me into a side hug.

I sigh, curling into his body, happy to be here with a teasing, fun, makeshift family. It's been a long time since I belonged somewhere.

CHAPTER NINETEEN

*A*fter some discussion and a lazy morning, we decide to get lunch out and then head over to Bellamy's previous residence to check on things since he didn't make it this morning after his donut run, and from there Fox is taking me on a matinee movie date. Bellamy borrows some of Fox's clothes since we basically kidnapped him, and I reluctantly wear some of my old clothes without my bling.

What I need is to get my ears pierced so Fox can buy me fancy earrings I can wear all the time. Yes, I know I would have to do the piercing myself, but I feel confident in my aim after injecting the chip into my hand. And it would be so worth it to have everyday diamonds in my ears.

The wall in front of the brownstone is lined with chattering gargoyles. The cacophony drowns everything out, but since their church bell voices are always in tune, it's not unpleasant to hear. I do stop and halt Bellamy's progress as well, looking to Fox for an interpretation of the chatter.

He bends his ear, listening for a moment, then shakes his head. "Gossip."

Feeling safe, I release Bellamy and take Fox's hand, following him past the gargoyles and the wards. As soon as we hit the sidewalk, an SUV drives up, unleashing a hail of bullets from both passenger windows.

Fear makes me do an insane jump in front of Fox and Bellamy. Bullets ricochet off my ward, flying off in all directions. The slugs riddle everything around me with holes, including some of the gargoyles. Their voices rise in volume, drowning out the rattatat of the gunfire. After a burst of gunfire only a few seconds long, the SUV zooms away in a squeal of tires and reckless driving.

The gargoyles follow in a cloud of bat wings.

I would not want to be the guys who just shot up our gargoyles.

Fox grabs my shoulder hard. I turn, looking him over as fury ignites in my soul. His chest took several shots before I got in front of him, his arms bleed from a few more, but what pisses me off is the hole in his cheek and the shattered teeth visible under the blood.

I am *so* going to enjoy walking in when it's Santanos' time to die.

Bellamy, thank heavens, is fine, and he helps me get Fox back behind the ward around the brownstone and onto one of the kitchen tables. Immortal or not, he's losing a lot of blood. Urgency to stop the bleeding moves me. I grab towels from the linen closet and bump my hip on every fucking corner of every fucking table between the hall and the kitchen. When I get back, Bellamy has cut away Fox's shirt and is halfway done with his pants. I drop the towels on the table and grab the first aid kit from under the kitchen sink and finally am able to stop moving long enough to start assessing how to help him.

Fox gazes up at the ceiling, pain pinching his face as I pick the hole bleeding the most and pinch the skin together. The first *ktchk* of the stapler makes me tear up.

"What are you doing?" Bellamy demands, grabbing the gun out of my hand. "You need to make sure there's an exit wound before closing the hole!"

"No," Fox rasps, spitting blood with every slurred word. "Just close it. Don't worry about the bullets."

I take the stapler back and finish closing the first hole up.

"What if they're blocking your arteries? They could give you a blood infection," Bellamy argues, while putting pressure on some of the worst bleeds now that he's denuded our patient.

"I'll absorb the metal. Can't get sick. Just close the wounds. There's a surgical needle and floss in the first aid kit." Fox reaches up and grabs my neck. "Gonna pass out now. Don't. Worry."

And with that, my man's eyes roll up and he goes limp.

Dammit. Don't tell your boyfriend not to worry when he's literally stapling your flesh together. It's just asking too much.

The thunderous crack of lightning outside startles me in the middle of pulling the trigger on the stapler and one of my staples goes wonky. Ten minutes ago, the sky was clear and the day warm, and now buckets of rain pour down in sheets outside the kitchen window. My next staple goes wonky because the front door unexpectedly slams open. It's a good thing Fox's scars fade because this one is going to be weird. No, I'm not taking the wonky staples out to try again; I'm barely hanging by a thread to get this much done.

"We're here!" Tag calls as he and Fox's other three fathers run into the kitchen. "Romily, give Dakota the stapler. Bellamy, give Amos the needle. Boys, go wash up. We'll have Arlington fixed up before you get back," he assures us, making sure we follow his orders and pushing us down the hall.

My stomach cramps at the thought of leaving Fox, but Tag walks me all the way to the master bathroom.

"Take a shower. Wash the blood off. Amos and Dakota will take care of Arlington. He's not dying. I promise. A few bullets are not enough to kill him, and even if they were, that just makes it harder to kill him next time."

What does that even mean?

I don't have my phone, and I can't ask, but Tag is smart. He kisses my forehead and murmurs into my skin, "We'll explain later. Immortality can be difficult. Just know, he's fine."

I give a stiff nod and Tag leaves me in the bathroom, closing the door behind him on the way. My hands shake as I attempt to undress, and it takes me a dozen tries to get a grip on my shirt long enough to pull it over my head. My brain is stuck in some kind of dazed loop, feeding me images of Fox's wounds and the pool of blood beneath him. I trust his athair's love for him; I know Fox is ok because Tag isn't in panic mode, but I can't stop the shaking.

Try as I might, I cannot get a grip on my jeans long enough to unbutton them, so I give up, collapsing onto the toilet lid. I grip my hair in my hands, sitting there for who knows how long before the bathroom door opens.

Bellamy crouches in front of me, clean with wet hair. He looks at me with sympathy and pulls me to my feet. Without filling the silence, he helps me out of my ruined clothes and into the shower. He washes the blood off me and out of my hair and then hands me a clean towel before stepping out of the bathroom.

I dry myself off and follow him out. He's put a pair of yoga pants on the bed and has one of Fox's shirts in his hand. "Get dressed. Fox is fine. Apparently he's immortal," he teases with a soft smile.

He leaves me then, and I spend a minute pulling Fox's clothes on before heading back toward the kitchen. The fathers waylay me, ushering me to the living room where Fox reclines on the sofa, cleanish, under a warm blanket, and pale but conscious.

I kneel next to him, frowning at him because he scared the shit out of me and I should never be in charge of first aid again. Clearly I do not do well with bullet holes and blood.

Fox puts his arm around my shoulders and pulls me into a snugglehug. Don't look at my word like that; it's a valid description. I reserve the right to make up important words.

"Since Arlington traumatized you two, I'm going to explain about the immortality thing before we leave," Tag says, pushing Bear into the recliner and sitting on his lap.

"I'm not traumatized," Bellamy protests.

"Your Oppa looked like he was dying; you're traumatized," Tag insists, waving off Bellamy's protest.

I am definitely traumatized, but still sans phone, so all I do is snuggle into Fox a bit more.

Tag interrupts Bellamy's next protest with his explanation. "Immortality doesn't preclude death. It makes us hard to kill, but we don't start out that way. In fact, one of the first things a new immortal should always do is die as many ways as possible. We let Arlington grow up before we started letting him die, but I've known immortal parents that use the first years of life to kill their kids."

"And I thought my parents were bad," Bellamy mutters, and I have to agree.

"It's a kindness. The babies don't remember dying when they're older, but they're protected from the worst ways to go. Think of it like getting a vaccine. There are only so many ways to die and an immortal can only be killed once by any method. Once you've been beheaded, you can never be beheaded again," Bear explains.

"Which is why most parents do the worst ways to die when their child won't remember it," Amos adds, shooting a disapproving frown at Tag.

"I couldn't kill my baby, and we have the advantage of a telepathic link, so any time Fox dies, we know it and can come put him back together again," Tag growls at his mate? Husband? Partner? At Amos.

"I died by firing squad in the late 1800s, so I wasn't going to die today," Fox mumbles.

"And even when he does, Arlington only stays dead for a few seconds unless he's dismembered. We have to put the pieces back together if he dies by losing his parts. Which is why we made sure he was dismembered in a controlled environment," Bear says, squeezing Tag in a hug that looks like it's to comfort the blue haired Fae; Tag's sympathetic smile says it's more for his partner's comfort.

"The closest I've ever come to permanent death was when I was blown up. I would truly be dead if Pater didn't have a good rapport with the hellhounds. It took three of them a week to find enough of me to resurrect," Fox adds, wincing a little at the tightness from the stitching holding his face together. The mumbling doesn't help his defense since I know it's the result of missing teeth and, you know, the whole bullet through the face thing. "The point is, even if I die, you know it's temporary and I can't be killed that way again."

I give him a flat expression, communicating as intensely as I can that it really doesn't make the close calls any less scary and that I am not cut out for first aid to bullet holes. I can watch, but I'll need a lot more practice to have stable hands for that shit, or better yet, he could just avoid getting hurt bad enough that he can't administer his own first aid.

Fox's eyes soften with affection, and he kisses my temple. "You're ruining the badass reputation of Harbingers everywhere by pouting."

I gasp at the insinuation that I should aim to do anything less than *set* the standard for the reputation for all Harbingers everywhere. Besides, exactly how badass can a Harbinger be when our magic only works if we're non-violent? Dammit. Now I need to meet these allegedly badass Harbingers that came before me.

I huff in frustration and make grabby hands to anyone with a device on them.

Amos tries to hand me a notebook and pen he pulls out of the front pocket of his nerd shirt. I flatten my lips at him and narrow my eyes, taking the damn writing tools. I point two fingers at my eyes, turn them to his eyes, then point to the paper.

My handwriting looks like a preschooler's as I scribble, *Does this seem like a good idea now???*

Amos' black eyes widen, and he takes the notebook back, replacing it with his phone with the notes app up. "Apologies, Harbinger."

I take the notepad back and point it around the room so everyone can see that I should never be allowed to actually write words by hand. I point to the notebook and then give everyone a warning glare and shake my head.

I get a hilarious number of mute nods in return.

How badass could your previous Harbingers have been if I'm the current one? I heard they all quit on you, and we both know I'm so deeply committed we're already planning our wedding. Well, Tag and that wedding planner are/will be. I think what you meant to say was that I'm setting the bar so high, every Harbinger that has ever come before me is weeping, knowing they will never achieve such greatness.

Fox blinks at the message, the corners of his lips turned up. "That's what I said," he agrees.

Tag sighs, drawing our attention to his sappy smile as Bellamy complains, "Are you going to let the rest of us in on the joke?"

I give him a bright smile and type out a message to him.

You can be my flower boy!

Bellamy scowls at the phone before his expression clears as he hands it back. "I'll be sure to let the cherubs know that you're passing them over for me."

Noooo! That's just manipulative and mean! Now I need the cherubs to be my flower throwers and ring bearers!

"What's he saying?" Bear asks, pushing Tag to grab the phone.

Dakota stomps down the hall, not angrily; he's just so big that stomping is in natural gait. "I'll get his phone so he can just group message us," he throws over his shoulder.

My heart settles into a happy beat, I've never had people committed to hearing me like this. I'm amazed at and love this family for wanting to know my words even though I can't speak them.

CHAPTER TWENTY

Daddy: I need you, Fox, and Bellamy in my office ASAP.

I stare at the message, squinting at the bright light of my phone in the darkness of Fox's bedroom. It takes me several long moments for the haze of sleep to clear enough for me to feel the urgency of Annette's message.

Me: **yawn* Do you need me functional or just present?*

Daddy: *I have coffee and a diamond bracelet.*

Me: *I'll be there as soon as I can.*

I turn back toward Fox, curling up behind him. And shaking him gently.

"We have one more day of paternity leave," he mumbles, pulling my arm over him.

Sly fox. I can't talk to him if I can't type, and he's facing away from me so he can pretend that I don't have anything to say. He's good, I'll give him that, but unfortunately when the Avatar of good summons you to her office, you damn well get out of bed at two a.m. and go to her office.

I nip Fox's shoulder, pinching the skin enough to make him release my wrist, and show him the message from Annette.

Fox stiffens in my arms and then rolls onto his back, turning to look at me. He studies my face and presses a chaste kiss to my lips. I linger there for a moment, then in tacit agreement, we haul ass out of bed, hurrying to get ready to leave.

Fox wakes Bellamy while I dress since it takes me ages to get into my suit and get my accessories in place. By the time I have my hair tamed, Fox and Bellamy are both waiting by the front door, ready to go. Bellamy's all black clothes don't surprise me; the fact that it includes a short, hooded cape sure does. I've stepped into a video game. One of my characters can carry more weight than an iron man and the other is one with the shadows.

I think that makes me the posh narrator with the British accent that hires the characters to go on an adventure to get the treasure or whatever. Fun.

This time when we exit the house, we look both ways before crossing the ward. Belaphor waits in his cab, which makes me wonder if I've somehow gotten a driver or a stalker. I'm pretty much ok with either since it means I have transportation waiting for me when I step out of my house.

Belaphor eyes the three of us and starts the meter. No one has to tell him where we're going, so I guess the depot hired him to be on call for me.

Fox pays for our ride when we get to the high-rise. Bellamy fidgets under his hood as we enter the building, tapping his free hand nervously against his thigh as we settle into the elevator. He carries with him a gun case *for his sniper rifle* that he leans against his hip as we head up to Annette's floor. I bend to catch his eye under his hood and pat his chest comfortingly; it's hard going into ex-enemy territory for the first time. Well, I assume so. I've never had enemies.

Bellamy frowns at me and brushes my hand off his chest, but he holds my hand until the last second, basically admitting that he needs his Papa's comfort.

The elevator lets us off on the thirtieth floor, and I grab Bellamy's wrist to walk him through the glass door leading into Annette's office. And holy shit. It's a circus in here. Bodies everywhere, people yelling, what looks like angry parents crowding the paralegal's desk. It's chaos, and the noise is just way too loud.

Fox takes one slow look around the room and lifts his hand to his lips, letting loose a sharp whistle that silences the room and stills the people milling about. Once he has everyone's attention, he lowers his hand and slowly swivels his blank mask so everyone can see him. "If you are not essential, go home. If you think you are essential but Mallory doesn't, go home. If you are essential, but don't want to be here. Go. The fuck. Home. Anyone lingering in five minutes will explain to my sword why their presence is essential."

Nothing inspires mass exodus like a good old fashioned death threat. It probably helps that the threat comes from Timothy Blackblade, aka Fox.

Within a few minutes everyone clears out from the waiting room, leaving the three of us and the paralegal behind her desk. She gives Fox a frazzled look. "Thank you. Annette is expecting you in the conference room."

Fox dips his chin and leads us back to the same cozy room where I initially met Annette. The room is empty, and Fox pulls me into his lap like he did the last time. Bellamy takes a seat next to us, sitting stiffly and leaning his gun case against his body between his legs.

I pat his shoulder as his gaze darts around the room. My boy is ridiculously uncomfortable, but he'll get over it.

Annette storms into the room, cigar hanging from her lips, scowling as she takes up the space across from us, leaning her butt on the table. She pulls the cigar out of her mouth and ashes it straight onto the floor. "Santanos is missing, and someone infiltrated the processing center where we were housing the cherubs and stole five of them right out from under us. We know that Santanos didn't take the cherubs; his people are in as much chaos as we are searching for him. They've asked us for help. The council has approved the request, so now we have to track down the cherubs and Santanos. I want you three to find the fucking Avatar and get him safely back to his people." She lifts her hands against some imagined protests, I'm sure. "I know. Whatever happened to him is probably a problem of his own making, but the council insists that we save that asshole, and you three have the best chance of finding him, better than any of the rest of my people. Bellamy, is Romily's ward working for you yet?"

Bellamy stiffens at his name and then nods. "Yes, most of the bullets from the attack this afternoon were aimed at me, but the ward deflected them."

My head spins toward him so fast, my brain bangs against my skull.

Bellamy glances at me and shrugs. "I accepted your claim."

"Which is good for us. You were quite the thorn in our side." Annette puffs on her cigar and points it at Bellamy. "I, for one, am glad you've defected; do not disappoint me."

The door opens and one of Annette's minions enters carrying a tray of to-go cups and a decanter of what better be coffee. He sets the tray on the table at Annette's elbow and exits the room.

Annette perks up, stands up from the table, and practically skips out the door without a word.

Fox sits me next to Bellamy and stands to pour three cups of coffee, doctoring mine perfectly before handing it to me. As he and Bellamy fix up their coffees, I sink into the heat and bitterness of mine, anticipating the caffeine jolt that I'll get from it.

"We should start with Gregory and Hassan; they're Santanos' main bodyguards. You saw them in action at the club," Bellamy suggests after getting his coffee and settling back next to me.

Fox takes up the space Annette abandoned as I bring out my phone because I really need words to participate in this conversation. My men almost absently take out their phones as well, making me grin as I start a group chat between the three of us.

Which ones were his bodyguards? There was a lot of sex going on. I assume that was a function of Santanos being an incubus?

"Incubus plus. Most incubaccha only feed on sex. They don't otherwise have much in the way of magical power. They're low on the totem pole of predators. Most can't even draw enough energy to kill a human; not like you see in pop culture. Santanos is one of the original four sex demons that were born from a pairing of the Lilith and Bacchus. He already had more power than the usual incubaccha, but then the council granted him more when they made him the Avatar of evil. He can use the power he draws from sex to cast spells, create wards, and other things I haven't been privy to witnessing."

So the orgy was just him powering up?

Also, my love, telling me Santanos is a hybrid plus doesn't really scream two powerful mythological beings that even I've heard of had sex and made baby Santanos. Next time feel free to elaborate.

"I didn't think it was relevant," Fox grunts.

Bellamy releases a long-suffering sigh; clearly he understands my frustration. "Anyway, yes, the orgy was a power draw for Santanos. Gregory was the one blowing him, and Hassan stood behind him. Their jobs are to keep Santanos brimming with magic. They're his bodyguards, and if someone actually took Santanos, they were there when it happened. They never leave his side."

Annette returns carrying two brightly colored gift bags. "I come bearing gifts for my sugar baby and grand sugar baby!" she announces, handing me and Bellamy one bag each.

"This is not the time, Annette," Fox disapproves quietly.

Annette pours herself a cup of coffee, scoffing at him as she takes it to her bar. "No time like the present for presents. Live in the moment, Fox."

As she adds a bit of Irish to her coffee, I rip the tissue paper out of my bag.

"Grand sugar baby?" Bellamy grunts, but let's all just notice how he doesn't hesitate to pull his tissue paper out of the bag. Look at him being a good grand sugar baby.

I pull out two gray shirts first. The top one says, "Him." The bottom says, "Me." I grin, tossing Fox's shirt to him and holding mine up so that Bellamy can't miss it.

Bellamy glares at his shirt, which reads, "Mini Me." Just like I wanted.

I add Annette to our group chat.

We're wearing these on our first family outing. Thank your grand sugar daddy for the lovely gift.

Bellamy stares at the shirt for a moment before reaching into his gift bag and pulling a velvet box out of it. I gasp and look in my bag, finding a matching box. When I open it, a gold chain sits attached to a delicate script on a gold plate with sparklies that reads, "Daddy's Favorite Me."

Bellamy growls, drawing my attention to an identical bracelet that reads, "Grandaddy's Favorite Mini Me."

God. I love this woman.

Bellamy grits his teeth at Annette. "I'm not calling you Grandaddy."

"Say 'thank you,' son," Fox responds without missing a beat.

Bellamy bares his teeth in a mock smile. "Thank you."

Annette's wicked grin makes me fall in love just that much more. "You're welcome."

Thank you, Daddy! We love your gifts!

Annette drops onto the couch next to me and helps me put the bracelet on, then pulls me into a hug, looking up at Fox. "What's the plan? I need to get back to finding our cherubs."

"We'll start with the bodyguards. Is he blocked from the council tracking?" Fox asks.

Annette grimaces. "Both his magic and his chip are blocked wherever he is."

I knew the chip was a tracking device.

Annette shrugs. "Obviously." She stands up and brushes her hand over my hair. "Find the other Avatar, boys. We really don't want to find out what kind of person the council would replace him with. The enemy you know and all that."

She takes her leave again, and for a few moments we all consider our next steps.

Bellamy gathers all of our presents into one bag and trashes the other and the tissue paper. "Santanos' home is hidden behind a dimensional ward. We'll have to get a minion to drive us in."

Do you know one who will cooperate?

"Belaphor does. Santanos owns half the cabs in this city."

Annette owns the other half.

Bellamy nods. "Yep."

Score two points for me.

CHAPTER TWENTY-ONE

A Reaper, a Harbinger, and an Acolyte walk into a bar...

Ok, it's the receiving room of a mansion as sprawling and ridiculous as my future in-laws' place. Still, the butler serves us drinks before leaving us alone to wait for Gregory and Hassan to join us.

When I try to bring my drink to my lips, the ward stops me. I glare at the tumbler and sit it down, shooting Fox a meaningful look. Fox pours my drink into his tumbler and then takes Bellamy's as well, scents it, and chugs all of it. "It's just cyanide," he explains.

I level my most deadpan expression at him.

No need to waste perfectly good liquor.

"Some of us aren't immune to poison and death," Bellamy mutters, stepping away from the poisoned tumblers.

"Yet," Fox replies. "We'll get you caught up on your immunizations."

I drop my jaw at Fox.

You're going to kill our son?

His eyes light up with laughter. "Multiple times."

"How exactly is that supposed to work? I'm not immortal. Not without Romily's magic."

Papa.

Bellamy doesn't respond.

Neither does Fox.

The stalemate lasts a whole minute before Bellamy capitulates to fate. "Not without *Papa's* magic."

Fox answers immediately. "My fathers will give you both immortality when we decide to retire."

Which ones? Or all of them?

"Omp and Pater. Omp could do it alone, but he would need the council's approval to do it. With Pater, it's a family matter that the council can't control."

"You're going to ask your parents to make me immortal?" Bellamy rasps out, bringing my scrutiny to his face because he's clearly gotten emotional about this.

"Yes," Fox confirms, watching our boy as intensely as I am.

Bellamy swallows a couple of times, white-knuckling the handle of his gun case. He looks between us before surrender takes over his features and he looks at the wall somewhere behind us. "Thank you."

Fox and I exchange a glance, but he doesn't really get it and I do; it's hard not to get emotional when someone offers you unconditional acceptance. In a private message to him, I let him know I'll explain later, then switch back to the group chat between the three of us.

Since they poisoned us, you think maybe they're not going to show up?

"They don't expect us to die. They just can't help themselves," Bellamy sighs, regaining his composure.

A few minutes later, Gregory and Hassan prove him right by showing up. Hassan looks pissed, while Gregory just looks suspicious.

"The council sent you?" Gregory demands, standing with his arms crossed and Hassan at his back.

"What happened?" Fox questions, ignoring his greeting.

Gregory scowls at him, but honestly the guy is so innocently pretty it just makes him look like an angry toddler. "Someone broke through the ward around our bedroom, hit us with a paralytic spell, and grabbed Santanos. They teleported out."

"Do you have a strong projector?" Fox asks, pouring more of the cyanide liquor (which smells like almonds, by the way—do you even know how awful it is that my favorite coffee flavor could get poisoned and I would never know it?) into his tumbler.

Hassan and Gregory both watch him imbibe, wide eyed, but say nothing about the cyanide.

Fox wipes his mouth, daring them with a blank mask to comment.

Gregory finds his voice first, which is fine since he seems to be the representative of the two anyway. "Uh, a projector? Yeah. We have a couple in house."

"Hassan, go get them, bring them to us in the room Santanos disappeared from. Gregory, lead us there," Fox orders, and whew, is it hot in here? That sexy commanding voice makes me want to find out what he sounds like giving orders in bed. Or taking them. Damn, that would be hot as hell.

I give Fox a *very* suggestive look, fanning myself because he should know he's hotter than the Fourth of July.

Fox flashes me a tiny smirk but has to wait on any real reaction when Gregory puffs up at his commands.

"What? You don't trust our *eyewitness* accounts? We told you everything."

Bellamy just fucking *moves*. One second he's standing in a half circle with me and Fox, and the next he's got Hassan pinned to the wall with the edge of a machete pressed up against Hassan's Adam's Apple. "I think it would behoove everyone under Santanos' command to just follow the orders of the men sent here to find him. You requested Annette's help; you were sent the most capable team. We could be finding the missing cherubs, we all would rather be finding those cute little fuckers, but we're here instead. Get the projectors, take us to your room, and let us get to work. And Gregory, unless we ask you a question, keep your damn mouth shut or I will occupy it with less courtesy than Santanos affords you. Understand?"

"Traitor," Gregory hisses.

And Bellamy slices Hassan's neck open.

Fuckityshitbitch.

Gregory gurgles as Hassan hits his knees, pressing his hands to his neck.

Bellamy swings his knife over to Gregory, putting the blade against his neck. "Did you think that a Harbinger claiming me would change my capacity for violence? Especially when that Harbinger made me the Acolyte of Arlington Fox, the Blackblade of Paris? Get the fucking projectors and take us to your room."

"You cut his throat!" Gregory cries, twitching to go to Hassan.

"Yes, I did. And if you cooperate instead of wasting time, he will only have a nice little scar to show for it. Shall we get on with this so you can administer first aid?"

Wow, Bellamy in professional assassin mode is scarily competent. He's totally going to end up being Annette's favorite minion. I'm not even jealous; I'm just really fucking proud of my boy.

Gregory whines and complains the whole time, but he also makes a couple of calls for people to meet him in the "master's bedroom" and leads us up to the third floor to a grandiose bedroom with a four poster platform bed big enough to fit fifteen people on it. It doesn't even take up a quarter of the room, which is nicely appointed even if the theme is torture—I mean sex. There's a St. Andrew's Cross, so I was probably right the first time.

Two people join us, a dragon lady with red scales, a long serpent tail, and green hair—she looks like a Christmas tree, and like someone who would eviscerate anyone stupid enough to say that aloud—and a beautiful young man with yellow eyes and orange hair.

I take up space holding up a wall while Fox starts instructing the minions.

"I want to see what happened physically first. Then show me what happened magically."

"Hurry up! Don't dawdle!" Gregory barks before either of the two minions can even blink.

The dragon lady hisses at him. "Go away, cocksucker," she rasps, voice brittle and charred like she's spent her entire life smoking.

"Don't you talk to me—"

"Out," Bellamy cuts him off, shoving him out the door. "Go tend Hassan."

Gregory jumps like he's been shocked by a cattle prod and runs out.

The dragon lady glares at Bellamy for a minute before turning to Fox. "I'm Calssandr of Agenamon, this is my apprentice Haigan Leafling."

Fox dips his chin in acknowledgment. "Are you here of your own accord or a slave?"

Calssandr scoffs. "Not even the prince of darkness can enslave a Draconian."

"But the Avatar of Evil may," Fox comments.

Calssandr grunts at that. "I'm here at the council's request." She waves a clawed hand at Haigan. "Project the physical."

Haigan nods and his smile brightens as he turns toward the center of the room and starts chanting under his breath. In a few moments, the room dims and the translucent forms of Gregory, Hassan, and Santanos appear on the bed. They're cuddled close, one bodyguard on each side of Santanos. He looks so sweetly innocent in his sleep, young and pretty. A few seconds later, a man pops into the room, masked like a ninja. His appearance disturbs all three men, and they're up before the masked man throws a vial of liquid over them. Immediately, Gregory and Hassan freeze in place.

Santanos says something, rolling off the bed to his feet, but this projection of the events is only visual, and I don't read lips, so I have no idea what he says. Then the masked man reaches out and just grabs Santanos. The shock on the Avatar's face reflects my own; the attacker got past his *ward*.

The masked man draws a line in the air and reality splits open behind Santanos. Without any ado, the masked man pushes Santanos backwards through the portal and follows him through. The portal closes and Gregory and Hassan come back to life.

"Now the magic," Fox urges, and we watch the whole thing again, this time with neon colors just fucking everywhere. The bedroom walls are bright orange, pink, and red, and then those colors blink out. Black smoke forms out of nowhere and the man pops into it. The liquid in the vial is bright blue. The words Santanos speaks fill the air with puce, and when the man breaches Santanos' ward, which flares blindingly bright white, he breaks it with a spear of steel gray that draws the white into itself. The portal he opens is black as pitch, and when he closes it, the black of the portal and the blue of the liquid in the vial disappear. The orange, pink, and red ward around the room doesn't reappear once he's gone.

We all stare in mute horror at what we just witnessed. The dude broke Santanos' ward.

Godfuckingdammit. Someone knows how to break the council's wards.

CHAPTER TWENTY-TWO

A silent conversation passes between Bellamy and Fox as they exchange a look. As awesome as I am at reading people, the only thing I get from their exchange is that they both know what we need to do now, and thank heavens for that.

Without a word, Bellamy unlocks his phone, taps it a couple of times, and lifts it to his ear. After a moment, he speaks with a subtle sort of affection in his genteel voice. "Hello, Darcy." I can't tell what the voice on the other end of the connection says, only that it's deep. "Just fine…Yeah, you heard right…I'm not sure yet…True. We need a tracker at Santanos' home… I'm aware…It's bad. Really bad…Broken council magic bad…Thank you." He ends the call and looks between me and Fox. "Darcy's a tracker. He'll be here shortly. I suggest Calssandr and Haigan leave. Darcy isn't Santanos' biggest fan. He will be antagonistic."

Calssandr scoffs and shakes her head, guiding her apprentice out without actually speaking words.

Bellamy shuts the door behind them and studies the room with a grim frown. "He'll get his *accoutrement* and pop in, since the wards aren't working and he can track me. He's…" he pauses, considering his words before continuing, "unreserved. He dislikes Santanos because they've clashed a number of times."

A pop crashes through the air as a tiny man of Asian descent appears, his spiked up, bottle-blond hair making him look like an anime character. He's several inches less than five feet tall and skinny like he could stand to eat several years of decent meals. The man is gothed-out with black make-up, a worn metal band shirt, more steel chains than any one person really needs, and a utility belt with satchels and tools hanging from it along with bulging pockets. He wears a worn black leather jacket over skinny jeans that display his assets prominently. Dude is hung and unashamed to show it off. He sneers at the room before his eyes land on Bellamy and a grin spreads on his raven-black lips. "Stepped in it this time, didn't ya, Red?" The voice on him matches his dick, so deeply bass it's a shock to hear it out of the tiny man, and it is as thickly country as an accent can get without coming straight out of the Ozarks. Actually, it might come from the base of the Ozarks.

"You know me," Bellamy hums, trying so hard not to eye-fuck the man. Blinking to clear the obvious lust on his face, he turns with a sweep of his arm. "This is Romily Butcher, Harbinger for Arlington Fox." He presents us both then uses his other hand to present his friend-he-wants-to-fuck. "This is Darcy Hellspinner, the best tracker to walk through the immortal realms."

"And that's no exaggeration," Darcy agrees, shaking first Fox's hand and then mine with a wink.

Fox studies the man for a moment as he pulls me under his arm, holding me close to stake his claim. I do so love his alpha possessiveness. "It isn't? I've never heard of you." He asks it matter-of-factly, not questioning the truth, merely curious why he doesn't already know Darcy.

"I try to stay out of council cock-ups," Darcy explains. "The problem with being the best is that everyone wants to own a piece of ya, and I value my independence too much to bend over and let the council fuck me." He gives Fox a salacious wink. "You on the other hand…"

The corner of Fox's lips twitch like he's suppressing a smile and his arm around me tightens just a miniscule amount. "I see. You came here to help us find Santanos. What do you think?"

Darcy's fists land on his hips as he spins to take in the room, switching to professional mode in a blink. "I think you got yourself a major fucking problem. Smells like death magic and hero-complex in here. You got yourself a necromancing Nephilim, and it ain't going to be an easy slide into a welcoming cunt to find him. I see where your necro-bastard portaled in and there's some shreds of his death magic up there where he tore through the ward," he points up to the ceiling and we all look up, but I immediately regret it because it's the Sistine chapel of porn where every face is Santanos's.

Gross.

"I didn't see that," Fox murmurs, staring up at the ceiling.

Bellamy glances up, but he looks just as disgusted as I am and quickly looks back down. "I can't see magic," he whispers to me, "and I wish I hadn't seen that."

I nod my whole-hearted agreement.

"Alrighty, let me get set up and we'll back-trace the death fucker, and if that leads to nowhere we'll follow the portal jumps, but that's not my first option. I'd rather see if we can find where he's been; might get lucky and find his homebase or at least something with enough of him seeped into it I can scry."

Darcy shakes out his arms and legs and pulls out a pointy athame that drips with that same gray ethereal smoke I saw during the demon fight.

I pull out my phone and my boys immediately follow suit, making me smile as I type into our group chat.

What's the gray smoke?

I'm guessing some kind of magic that makes the blades special somehow. It's a half point kind of guess, but I'll round up if I'm even in the same hemisphere as correct.

Fox follows my gaze to the athame and explains. "It's the magical pollution the blade filters out of the wielder. The blade can only use a certain kind of magic, and in the hands of a hybrid, it filters out the magic it can't use and purifies the magic it can. My blade filters out all the natural magic it takes from me and leaves only my demon magic."

"I'm not inherently magical, but mine draws the magic I absorb through my work and filters it down to earth magic," Bellamy adds.

Darcy shoots us a wicked smirk as he uses the athame to slice his wrist open. "Mine uses blood magic, but it has to filter out the hearth witch and fire dancer to get to the good stuff."

I really need a dictionary of species for this job. Is he talking about actual fire dancing like what you see in those Hawaiian performances on YouTube?

I've only seen it one time when one of the other kids in the home I was in showed us all a dance competition that included fire dancers.

"Human fire dancing evolved from shaman rituals," Bellamy answers.

Darcy looks between the three of us but doesn't say anything as he starts drawing a circular array of symbols around him in his own blood. Not a little blood, and the fat drops from his wrist don't appear to bother him; they cause the symbols to run and bleed—laugh at my punniness!—as he turns in a circle.

Once he finishes, he waves us over to him with that mischievous smirk on his lips. "Come on then, once I activate it, it'll move us along the traces of the necro magic. Brace yourselves, I'm not cleaning the puke off my shoes. First person to lose it will get that privilege."

I grimace, following my men into the circle with Darcy. Fox pulls out his sword, Bellamy hands me his gun case and unsheathes his machete, and Darcy throws some glitter into the air. Ok, it's probably not glitter, but I don't know what it actually is, and as soon as it reaches the zenith of its upward trajectory, the world suddenly lurches. Or rather we lurch upward, standing on a platform made of light held together by the magic of the array.

Panic jump starts my heart as we rush the ceiling, but before it can fully form we pass through to the room above and then the roof. We fly so fast the scenery blurs. My stomach revolts, so I slam my eyes shut, surprised to find that as long as I'm not looking, it feels like I'm standing still.

After a few minutes, Bellamy and Fox both take in a sharp breath, and of course, I stupidly open my eyes. We've slowed down in front of a familiar high-rise, and then we zip back to the brownstone, then all over the city. The most remarkable thing is that we keep going where we've already been, places where Fox has killed people, back to the brownstone several times, retracing our steps from the last few days, though not perfectly. It's like we're taking the scenic route sometimes and the direct route others. We end up at the high-rise and the brownstone most often, but when we end up outside of Sybillant, the restaurant where Fox and I had our first date, I smack Darcy's arm a couple of times to stop the ride.

Darcy doesn't interpret me fast enough and we're already retracing the path Fox and I took that day, ending up at the apartment complex where I was squatting before Darcy stops the spell.

I glare at him and type a quick message.

Now we're an hour and a half from home and I figured it out in front of Sybillant. You're paying the cab fare back home.

Darcy scoffs and the world slides out from under us, moving us to the sidewalk in front of the brownstone. "I'll pay for a cab when the lake of fire burns out."

"Why did we come home?" Bellamy asks as I walk up to the gargoyles guarding the gate.

I don't get fed up with my disability often, but as soon as I realize that I have no way of knowing if the gargoyles can read, I make a frustrated noise in my mouth, typing out to the group message what I need someone to ask the gargoyles.

Ask them if they know where Belaphor hangs out when he's not driving me. Someone tell me who to ask for his contact information, especially his employment information. Belaphor is the only person besides me who took a bunch of those routes, and he's transported me to every jobsite we went to twice under Darcy's spell.

"The cabbie," Fox growls, putting a hand on one of the gargoyles.

Church bells ring out from the gargoyle then Bellamy pulls me over to Darcy, phone ringing on speaker.

The phone clicks, but no one speaks, and Bellamy starts talking. I guess he trusts that someone is listening. "Belaphor Betelgeuse, ID number four-two-eight-four-white. Home address and a map of his pings in the last week overlapped with Arlington Fox's and Romily Butcher's. Urgent. If you have a ping on him right now, I need it."

There's some typing, then a robotic voice responds. "No ping. Information incoming."

Bellamy hangs up his phone, in full professional mode. He checks his email when it chimes and pulls up the map of Belaphor's location pings from the last week. The majority of the dots from the three of us overlap starting the day I was chipped, and before Fox hired me, Belaphor's pings overlap with Fox's; Belaphor was at the diner *and* the library. Damn.

I look up the only other place he pinged at regularly and discover it's the taxi garage. I'm not sure that's helpful unless he has a blackhole there he can step into when he's not driving his cab. I mean, the garage is kind of a blackhole; every day between four and five it opens up and swallows the taxis and then shoots them back out. It's kind of a crazy phenomenon, so it might be the center of some paranormal mystery.

I show Bellamy my phone and he cusses. "Hell. That's Santanos' garage. Yeah, let's go there."

Fox strides back to us with stress around his eyes. "They noticed him around, but assumed the depot sent him to be your personal driver. They weren't overly concerned with him, but they're spreading the word now; if any gargoyle around the city sees him, they'll let us know."

I send a grateful smile and wave to the gargoyles, then show Fox the garage where we need to head.

Would the depot make one of Santanos' cabbies my driver?

Fox vocally grumbles. "Yes. The cabs are owned by Annette and Santanos on paper, but they have to follow the rules of neutrality the council has set. Same for the depot. They would not have considered who he worked for as a reason not to assign him as your driver, especially if he requested the position."

I press a chaste kiss to his lips because I don't know what to say about that.

"Y'all are sweeter than honey pie, but if you don't mind, could we just pop on over to the garage? If we can find anything that he's touched, I can track his magic through any dimension or realm. There's nowhere he'll be able to hide from me. And add me to your fucking text conversation. And next time lead with 'the Harbinger is mute,'" Darcy interrupts, punching Bellamy's arm.

I wag a stern finger at Bellamy as he adds Darcy to our chat thread with a middle finger emoji.

Next time lead with "My papa is mute."

Darcy chokes as Bellamy, my red-headed adoptee, turns the color of a tomato under his freckles. "That is never happening," he rasps, nearly squeaking.

Fox chuffs next to me. "It just occurred to me that I'm going to have a red-headed step-child." He turns to me with amusement twinkling in his dark hazel eyes. "I'm probably going to marry you just so I can say that."

I nod, completely understanding where he's coming from.

I'd do the same.

"Jesus fucking Christ," Darcy laughs, bending at the waist to slap his leg.

Bellamy turns a deep shade of red, fisting his hands before letting out a slow breath and clearing his expression. "You are the most embarrassing pseudo-parents ever."

Thank you, son.

Bellamy shakes his head. "That was not a compliment, *Papa*."

Darcy sniggers, leaning on Bellamy and holding his stomach. "Oh gods. Y'all." He shakes his head without completing that thought, stands up, composing himself in a single moment, and looks up at all of us. "Ready?"

CHAPTER TWENTY-THREE

I think maybe that Bellamy might have understated things with Darcy when he called him "unreserved." Darcy storms into Santanos' taxi garage with a thundering clap of displaced air that damn near deafens me as he "pops" us all into the center of the garage.

Darcy's booming voice echoes through the huge space as soon as we land. "HELLO MINIONS! GET ME BELAPHOR BETELGEUSE, AND I WON'T SIC THE FOX ON YA!"

For several ridiculously long seconds everything in the garage goes quiet. We're well past the shift change at this point, but the place is still busy, hopping with the activities that keep a cab company running. Every employee/minion in the place turns to look at the tiny little Asian guy with a country accent and goth gear and a voice that wouldn't be out of place on a phone sex line. I mean, I could probably get off listening to him if he was dirty-talking me.

"What is wrong with you?!" A screech from above has us all looking up toward an actual harpy in flight, coming straight for us. She's got a pretty human half, huge tits hanging out, and the glossiest black wings I've ever seen. "GET BACK TO WORK!" she yells at the minions, alighting in front of us and shifting into a fully human form, dressed in coveralls with a clipboard in hand. Huh. Her magic shifts clothes onto her human form and includes a clipboard but leaves her harpy form buck naked.

I look up at Fox curious, pointing to the woman.

Fox shakes his head, and I sigh. I guess he's not part harpy, but I hear those creatures are only female, so I didn't think it was a good guess anyway.

"Belaphor Betelgeuse you say?" she questions, voice craggy like she misspent her youth running up the stairs in horror movies.

"I sure did, ma'am," Darcy replies, suddenly sounding like sex on a ministick.

I eye him as he takes a step closer to the harpy with a ridiculously charming smile on those black lips.

The harpy doesn't stand a chance in hell of resisting the man and licks her lips as she looks him over. He's a foot shorter than her, but damn, the charisma coming off him almost snags me.

"His last shift was last night. He put in his two weeks and worked doubles every day. He just turned in his car this morning."

"Do you mind letting me have a little look at his car? I just need to use it for a few minutes. I'm Darcy Hellspinner, by the way," he offers her his hand.

"Rowan Cran," she flutters, taking his hand and letting him kiss the back of it.

"Pleasure, Miss Cran. Competent and successful people are my kryptonite. Perhaps after I track down your employer, you wouldn't mind me tracking you down?"

Holy. Shit.

I shoot my gaze at Bellamy, who looks like he's suppressing the grimace from eating a lemon, and my empathy for him wells up. Fox and I move at the same time, each taking up one side of our Bellamy. Fox puts his hand over Bellamy's shoulder and I take his waist, and we just snugglehug him while we watch the trainwreck that is Darcy Hellspinner make mincemeat out of our boy.

Rowan chuckles at Darcy's charm and nods. "I wouldn't mind that one bit, Mr. Hellspinner."

"Call me Darcy, love," he offers, crooking his elbow at her like she's not covered in questionable stains and isn't a foot taller than him.

Rowan doesn't even blink; she puts one hand on his elbow and leads him (and the rest of us chumps) to a car in the line to get detailed.

"Oh love, this is wonderful. Thank you," Darcy says, running a hand over the hood of the cab. "I'll be done in a shake."

"Come find me when you are," Rowan flirts.

Darcy turns a heated look up at her. "I assure you, I will."

With that, the woman shifts back into her harpy form and takes off. Darcy watches her fly away and shoots us a lascivious wink. "Never bedded a harpy before." The lust clears off his face at the neutral masks we're all wearing, and he turns back to the cab, returning to his work voice, which admittedly is just as sexy as his lusty voice. "Let me get his scent and we'll find him."

Darcy opens the cab door and bends at the waist, audibly sniffing the driver's seat. Then he licks it. Twice. Gross.

Fart mouth. You dodged the bullet with that one.

I don't send that; I just hold it up where my boys can see it.

Bellamy barks out a laugh. "I wish."

What? Did he already fuck you?

Bellamy purses his lips and lets out a slow breath, nodding once.

It's totally hypocritical of me to judge you, but I am. 100%

Bellamy chuckles as Darcy stands and turns back to us. "Got the bastard. Let's go. ROWAN, I'M ABOUT TO MAKE A BLOODY MESS."

"NOT IN MY CAB!" She screeches back from somewhere in the garage.

"NEVER, LOVE! ON THE FLOOR!"

"I'VE GOT POWER WASHERS!"

"THANK YOU!"

"Aren't you worried that someone will get your blood?" Fox murmurs.

Darcy shakes his head. "I've got it spelled to reflect any magic done to it back on the caster. The only beings capable of using my blood against me are actual blood gods, and I have an understanding with every last one of them." As he explains this, he cuts his wrist open along the scab of the previous wound and starts drawing another array of symbols on the floor.

This time instead of a circle, he draws in two parallel lines about three feet apart that run the length of the car.

We watch in silence until he finishes drawing, looking a bit more pale than he had before. He walks to the back of the cab and pulls a pinch of the glitter out of one of the pockets on his utility belt and tosses it down the line of the array, activating the magic.

"Decide what order you're going in. Walk between the lines; when you step past the end, you'll be stepping into the room with the largest concentration of the necro-Nephilim magic, which should be where he is if he isn't storing his power in artifacts."

Fox's eyes tighten with worry when he looks at me. "He can break your ward, but this is official business."

And officially Harbinger's go before their Reapers, which makes this a dangerous job for me.

Good thing I have an assassin Acolyte.

"On your heels," Bellamy assures me, pulling out his machete again (he decided to leave the sniper rifle at home).

Fox looks like he's trying to swallow nails, so I step up to him and press a kiss to his lips. When I pull back I exaggerate mouthing, *Love you.*

His hand on my hip squeezes me. "You're so bad at that," he teases softly, pressing his forehead to mine. "Love you too. Run if he tries to grab you."

I kiss him again and nod, heart fluttering at his love confession. Even if we never get that third date, I'm fucking him when this is over. I've stuck to the plan long enough for it to go wrong twice; I'm not waiting another night.

He releases me, and I jerk my head for Bellamy to follow. I thank Darcy with a punch to his shoulder and put some steel in my spine before walking down the line.

I feel the magic thicken as I walk. On one side, it's like strolling through air, but as I reach the middle, it's more like wading through soup, and it gets thicker as I get to the end of the array, like pushing through gravy. Yeah, sorry; I'm hungry. It's way past breakfast, and the coffee's already passed through.

When I step past the end of the line, I literally come out the other side nose to nose with Belaphor. Reacting on instinct, I push him away and dodge to the side. Belaphor stumbles back three paces and hits the edge of a table where he has Santanos strapped down.

Bellamy walks in immediately, finding me and stepping to my side, holding the machete at the ready, facing Belaphor.

Belaphor laughs, reaching back to put his hand on Santanos' chest. "Welcome, Harbinger and your Acolyte. I assume your Reaper is—Ah, there he is."

Fox appears, pointing his sword at Belaphor.

Santanos screams.

Visible, puce magic curls up from Santanos' chest, swirling around Belaphor's arm and diving into his chest. Fox runs at him, swinging his sword, but the magic flares, sending the sword bouncing off a ward and out of Fox's grip.

Shit. He's using the council's ward. We need to get Santanos away from him.

"Can't kill what the council wants alive, can you?" Belaphor taunts with a wide grin. "They want the Avatar alive, but they don't actually care who the Avatar is, do they?" He looks over at Santanos with a creepily affectionate gaze. "Give me a few more hours and I'll be the Avatar we need. Santanos is weak. Always submitting to the whims of the council. He should have had a bit more backbone. The balance is never in our favor because the council is biased, isn't it? I'm going to change things for my people." He turns a sharp glare on Fox. "You won't be killing my people so much when I become the Avatar."

"Lord save us from self-important minions," Darcy's dry voice startles us all. I didn't even notice his arrival. He carries a bowl in one hand while his other one stays busy pulling ingredients out of the pockets and satchels of his utility belt and adding them to the bowl. "Fox, it occurred to me that this fucker knows the trick to breaking the council's wards, and then it occurred to me that you probably don't, so I came to help out a bit."

His busy hand stops, and he shakes a couple of drops of blood from his wrist into the bowl.

Belaphor sneers at him. "The only way to break the ward is to absorb it."

Darcy snickers as he tosses the contents of his bowl toward Belaphor.

Neon green, blood red, and fiery orange magic flares up as soon as it hits the ward, and we watch the magic of the borrowed ward melt off Belaphor.

Santanos' screams quiet to whimpers and the draw of magic out of him ceases.

"Your turn, Reaper," Darcy announces and falls back to Bellamy's side.

Fox doesn't even twitch, he just *moves*. I've watched him fight hand-to-hand, but there's usually weapons involved in those fights. This time, he attacks unarmed. The two of them are a blur to watch, and honestly, I can't follow the furious flash of their fists and kicks. They're both very good at hand-to-hand combat, but this isn't Hollywood where everything is scripted and choreographed for film. It's a fight, and it's difficult to keep up with, and they move too quickly for me to see. Just imagine Keanu Reeves in the *Matrix* fighting Mr. Smith, but you know, no slowy-downy parts.

What? That's a legitimate descriptive-word technique for the verbal, why can't I use it? Don't be prejudiced against the nonverbal. We can add the ee sound too. We just can't make the ee sound.

Belaphor is about a match for Fox in speed and strength, which begs the question:

I thought the Nephilim were giants?

I send that in the group chat that includes Darcy.

Darcy and Bellamy both pull out their phones and check my message.

"They've been bred down to normal size. The originals were around twenty-five feet tall. Crazy big. But rumor has it they had small dicks since they were able to breed human women," Darcy snickers. "Rumor also has it, today's Nephilim still have small dicks." He says that loud enough for Belaphor to hear him.

We don't dick-shame in our family. All dicks are beautiful.

Darcy winks at me. "Nothing to be ashamed of in your family."

I have not been naked in front of this man, but, ahem, Fox's fighting always turns me on, and my suit isn't designed to hide my assets; Darcy isn't shy about looking at my crotch.

Oh hey, look at that, Fox got his elbow around Belaphor's neck.

And now he's on the floor, flipped over Belaphor's shoulder.

Santanos is looking a little pale.

JENNIFER CODY

Should we do something about the Avatar? I mean, we could probably take him while Fox is keeping Belaphor busy.

Bellamy considers this while Darcy outright dismisses it.

"I'm not touching that fucktard," Darcy grunts.

Bellamy's expression says he agrees with Darcy. "It's a risk to touch him. If he's in need of power, his magic will lash out. I don't really want his magic making a mess in my pants again."

Ugh. Yeah, no thanks. Any way we can get his minions to come retrieve him?

"Sure, but we need to know where we are."

We both look at Darcy, who shrugs. "GPS on your phones should work. We haven't crossed dimensions."

I leave the details to Bellamy, but I do check over his shoulder where we are. Huh. Nova Scotia. Odd place to set up camp.

The fighting noises suddenly stop, bringing my attention to where Fox stands over Belaphor's body, head turned the wrong way. He points at the man. "That's an immortal."

"Shit," Darcy cusses and quickly grabs his athame off his belt, running to the body and stabbing Belaphor through the ear. "Ok, he's down for now. I want my athame back when you get him secured."

"I'll make sure you get it," Fox agrees, picking the body up and heading out the only door into the room.

Bellamy pushes me to follow. I guess we're leaving Santanos tied to a table. Can't say I'm sad about that.

CHAPTER TWENTY-FOUR

*F*ox leads us with unerring accuracy through the building, up a flight of stairs, and out a steel door into a grassy flatland overlooking the ocean. The door is set in a hillock and clearly leads to an underground bunker. I wouldn't even mention it, but damn, this place is beautiful. Have you seen pictures of Nova Scotia? I haven't, but now I don't have to look them up. It's gorgeously green here, the ocean crashes against the cliffs a hundred feet in front of us, and beyond that, the blue-gray water goes on forever, making me feel small and insignificant in a good way. Sometimes it's good to remember that you're just a tiny part of the universe as a whole. A blip. It makes what you do now that much more important.

Fox drops Belaphor in the grass and looks to Darcy. "You finished out your contract and found Santanos; send me the bill through the depot. It would be convenient for you to transport Romily and Bellamy home while I deal with this." He waves over Belaphor's body. "And I'll bring your athame with me when I return."

I look up at Fox curiously while Darcy replies.

"I'll do it. No problem."

Fox gives him a nod of acknowledgement and pulls me by my hips into his body. "There's a prison for immortals north of here. I'll fly him there and be back as soon as I can."

I tap the wings on his back, curious if I'm about to witness what their function is.

He nods. "Yeah. But maybe you should make your last guess before I shift."

Oooh, a shifter! Ok, a shifter with wings. Probably big since his omp is massive. Something with electricity. Possibly lightning and thunderstor—

Fuck. I should have figured it out already. I even recently read a book with this kind of shifter in it. Dammit.

Thunderbird, right?

Fox beams at me. "Sassy, beautiful, and smart. I'd marry you even if you didn't come with a red-headed step-child."

I laugh and press my face into the crook of his neck, blindly typing out my next message.

I ducking love you.

Eh. Autocorrect got it mostly right.

Fox chuffs at the message and kisses me, swiping his tongue along mine for too short a time before stepping back. He gives me a wink and starts stripping off his weaponry, handing me the belts and holsters. He notices his empty sheath for his sword and sighs. "Will you grab my sword before you leave?"

I nod, straining to hold up the weight of his weapons. Steve Rogers I am not.

He gives me one last kiss and then runs full out toward the cliff. He jumps when he reaches the edge, spreading his arms as he falls over. A deafening boom echoes up from the cliffs, then a massive white bird shoots up. Huge. The size of a small plane.

Fox in his thunderbird form is…magnificent. Lightning crackles off his beak in a spiderweb of flashes as he gains altitude. He spreads his glorious white wings as he soars, banking to turn toward us, huge yellow-orange talons extended.

I stumble backward, retreating so that I'm not in his way when he dives for Belaphor's body, staring up at my…everything. Damn, he's beautiful, sexy, competent, funny—everything a man could ever hope for. I'm so fucking lucky.

Fox swoops in, grabbing Belaphor up and knocking us all on our asses with the backdraft from his wings as he flies upward with his prisoner and turns north.

I can't help it; I stare until I can't see him. Only when my eyes are just playing tricks on me, trying to convince me that I can still see him, do I look back to my companions. They're in conversation, discussing Fox's sword, which Bellamy holds between them, as they examine it closely. He's kneeling so he can hold it up to his eye level and Darcy can bend to get the same point of view. They're within kissing distance, and if it wasn't for Darcy's blatant disregard for Bellamy's crush on him, it would be cute.

Who am I kidding? It is cute.

I pull up my phone, take a picture, and send it to Annette.

Me: *Our boy's first crush.*

Daddy: *He should see the demon sword. It's way more crush-worthy.*

Me: *I'm actually talking about the twink with a baseball bat between his legs.*

Daddy: *Pics or it doesn't exist.*

Me: *I'll get one for you. Did you find the cherubs?*

Daddy: *I did not. *rage emoji**

Me: *Darcy can track anything.*

Daddy: *Make him an offer.*

I snap my fingers at the boys, drawing their attention, and shove my phone into Darcy's face, letting him read the text conversation.

Darcy hands me back my phone. "I need twenty-four hours to rejoice, but I'll help. Why didn't you put me on that first? I'd much rather find the kids than the fuckhead."

"Annette's orders," Bellamy replies, sliding the sword into its sheath.

"The other fucking Avatar." Darcy seems to hold as much disdain for Annette as he does for Santanos.

"Minions do what we're told. The cherubs were abducted from the processing center," Bellamy explains as I text Annette back.

Me: *He needs 24 hrs. to recover from finding Santanos, but he'll help.*

Daddy: *Good. Who is he?*

Me: *Darcy Hellspinner. The best tracker in the immortal dimensions and that's no exaggeration.*

Daddy: *He's shorter than I expected.*

Me: *Everything about him is a surprise, trust me. He charmed the pants off a harpy right in front of me.*

Daddy: *That's actually impressive. Harpies are notorious misandrists.*

Me: *She invited him for sex after we found Santanos. Also, if harpies hate men, why the hell would she be working for Santanos?*

Daddy: *Not all harpies are the same. Some are evil and equal opportunity.*

Me: *So many questions.*

Daddy: *AMA.*

Me: *Later. I need food and sleep.*

I switch to the group message with Darcy.

Home. Food. Sleep. And a naked picture of your cock.

"Done," Darcy agrees, grabbing both of our wrists and popping us from the bunker to the brownstone. Well, outside the brownstone.

Seriously, how has magic not been discovered by humans yet? We just popped into existence. On a public sidewalk. During rush hour. How? How has no one noticed magic? We're not subtle at all.

I pat my gargoyle friends on the way by and head up to the front door. By the way, Fox is one of those crazy people who doesn't lock his doors because he relies on his ward and reputation to keep his space safe. I'm not even sure he knows where his keys are.

If I was a thief, I'd totally scope out his place after watching me walk in the front door without unlocking it. I wouldn't succeed because of the ward, but I would try.

And we all know wards can be broken. Belaphor proved that.

Shudder.

That makes me feel less safe. Who knows how many people he told how to get past the council's wards? Right now, I'm grateful for Bellamy's skills and that I stole him from Santanos. Also, Darcy knows how to break the council's magic, and that concerns me just as much as Belaphor knowing.

I lead Bellamy and Darcy to the kitchen and point out the breakfast nook window to the back garden, shoving Bellamy toward the backdoor. We need a healthy breakfast scramble, and someone needs to scatter some seed for the sparrows.

Bellamy arches a brow at me and smirks, stopping in his tracks. "I'm not a mind reader."

I drop my shoulders and give him a very expressive flat look, challenging him to defy me. I have zero problem embarrassing him again; I hear that's what parents are supposed to do.

His cocky attitude wavers after a long ten seconds, then as I reach for my phone, the man suddenly realizes that he would probably prefer going out to the garden rather than finding out what I might say, and he hightails it to the backdoor.

I would have totally embarrassed him.

"You're exceptionally skilled at nonverbal communication," Darcy notes, studying me from his perch on the kitchen table. Not the one in the breakfast nook. This one is in the actual kitchen.

I give him a sly smile and a wink then open the fridge to grab enough veggies for a breakfast scramble.

"So, what's with all the tables?" he asks after a minute.

I look at him, look down at my full hands, and back to him again, blinking at him like he's stupid. I know he's not but filling the silence with not-yes-or-no questions is dumber than a mute boy. I can say that; it's my disability, and I can be as un-PC as I want to be when it's convenient for me.

Darcy laughs as I prep the cutting board and knife. "Ok, yeah, that was stupid of me."

I nod. Emphatically.

"Do you know why there are a crazy hoarder number of tables?"

I don't, so I shake my head. I was waiting for our third date to ask. Sigh. I'm going to get my third date. It's as inevitable as the next ice age, but maybe as far away as that.

Darcy clearly doesn't know the meaning of silence is golden, because the man starts talking, and if I didn't have some kind of aural fixation on his voice, I'd probably find it annoying. Unfortunately, he has a nice voice, so I let him fill the air with it.

"There's this old man in the Arkansas Ozarks that I've met a couple of times. He's just this crazy hermit guy that everyone in the area talks about in rumors. Anyway, he's human but so old that most people think he's a ghost or just a tall tale. Occasionally a tourist or hiker will spot the old mountain man and get a blurry picture. It's entertaining for everyone. Anyway, I asked him how old he was, and he told me that he shared a birthday with *Rube Goldberg*. You know, the guy who invented the crazy contraptions that do useless shit? I looked it up and that guy was born July 4, 1883. The old mountain man is still alive. If he isn't lying, and the dude looks old as fuck, he's pushing a hundred and forty years old…"

And on. It's interesting information, but he's just talking to fill the silence, so there's no point to it. My disability makes some people uncomfortable. Confidence is sexy, and my estimation of Darcy's sex appeal is dropping by the word.

Man needs to learn that trying to make up for my silence is the equivalent of telling me that there's something wrong with me, and that's just offensive. I have it on good authority that I'm perfect. Fox told me so.

It takes forever, and I'm well into sautéing the vegetables, but Bellamy finally returns with his harvest. I turn to give him my *finally*-look and freeze.

Oh my god.

He scowls at me as he tosses the vegetable onto the counter. His hair and shoulders are covered in wet spots of bird shit. I press my lips together as tight as I can, trying to suppress my laughter. He looks so mad. So very, *very* mad. Furious. Red-faced fury that just keeps getting darker the longer I stare at him.

"Did you know that sparrows are like crows and will shit bomb you for no reason?" he asks with a deceptively mild tone.

I slowly shake my head, pressing my lips into the tightest line I can make them. I can't do anything about the mirth in my eyes, but I make an effort because I actually need Bellamy to save me from Darcy.

Although, from the looks of it, he needs a shower more than I need saving.

With one hand, I type a message to him, deliberately leaving Darcy out.

In the future, we can leave the outside chores for Fox. Will you please show Darcy where to freshen up? I might accidentally stab him if you don't. You can use the master bathroom to clean up. The shower in there is nicer.

Bellamy's fury dissipates as he reads my words, and he shoots Darcy a totally noticeable surprised expression before looking back at me. "Sure."

I smile at him and find a place on him that isn't covered in shit to pat.

You're the best son ever.

He glowers at me, but since I didn't send that in a group text, he can't be mad at me for embarrassing him.

CHAPTER TWENTY-FIVE

I wake up hot and sprawled across Fox's bare chest. I swear that little puddle in the dip of his abs is sweat, not drool, and no one will ever get me to confess otherwise.

I don't know when he got back, but I'm proud of myself for making him cuddle me in my sleep.

I use the sheet pooled at his hips to wipe my mouth—what?—and peek below it because I'm not a good enough person to ignore the woody poking up. The man has a beautiful cock; I'll give him that. Even if it's totally weird he doesn't have balls. Not that his having internal testes bothers me, it's just not something you see every day, amiright?

His dick twitches as I stare, and I force myself to remember that we haven't talked about consent yet and what's ok and what's not. That's what date three was going to include, but of course it's not like we've gotten that far despite both of our efforts. I took a sexcation and he took paternity leave, and we still haven't managed enough time off to have our third date.

"Rethinking your three date protocol?" Fox murmurs, stretching out his hand to grab his cock, giving it a lazy pull.

I may or may not have to wipe my mouth on the sheet again. Has anyone in the history of ever actually had their mouth water at the sight of a nice juicy cock, or am I trailblazing?

Fixated on the way his hand moves over his shaft, I forget that he asked me a legitimate question until his other hand starts kneading my ass. Tired of holding up the sheet, I toss it over his hand and cock, watching him stroke himself as my own dick weeps for attention.

Fox jerks suddenly and his abs contract as he lifts his shoulders off the bed. "What—?"

His hand moves from his dick to his ribs, swiping through the pool of *sweat* that might have started dripping down his side.

"Did you drool on me?"

I sit up, giving him my widest, most innocent eyes and shake my head like I have no idea what he's talking about.

He reaches for the sheet and pulls it up, miraculously finding a damp spot on it. "Did you drool on me and then use my sheet to only clean up your face?" he questions suspiciously, using the sheet to wipe the sweat away.

I nod and shake my head both and end up just turning my face in a circle.

He finishes wiping himself down and pulls me back down onto his chest. "Would you like for me to finish?"

Why is that even a question?

I kiss his chest and wave my hand toward his dick, encouraging him to continue like we weren't interrupted by questionable body fluids.

Fox squeezes my butt and takes his cock back in hand, teasing himself as much as me as he pumps his shaft in slow strokes, gathering the drops of precum as they seep up. On every downstroke, he pulls the foreskin back just enough to make it a peek-a-boo show that has me sliding my hand into my underwear. The tension in him builds up with every measured stroke, and I match his pace on my own dick until the need becomes too much for both of us.

I'm not sure who breaks first, but my hand jerks faster, and he thrusts up into his fist, and then it's a race of the *schlick-schlick* of our hands shuttling up and down our cocks. The digits on my ass squeeze hard as his rhythm stutters, setting off my orgasm with a starburst of pleasure. Cum erupts from his cock, flowing rather than shooting, an erotic fountain of creamy white seed.

Panting and melty from the lovely orgasm, I wipe my hand on the dirty sheet and cuddle into Fox, kissing his neck and resting there with my nose pressed into the sleepy, sexy, scent of him.

Fox wipes himself up with the sheet as well and then tosses it off the bed and pulls the comforter up over us. For a while we just cuddle without the need to fill the void of silence. It's nice and relaxing, and when we do eventually stir, because needs must be attended to, we're both content with the time we've spent together and the shared intimacy.

We take turns in the bathroom, and after he steps out of the shower, I hand him his phone, which has a message from me waiting for him.

Come tell me while I shower what happened after you flew off yesterday.

Fox obediently follows me into the bathroom and starts talking as I disrobe and get into the shower. He even makes the effort to speak over the noise of the water.

"I told you that I was taking him to a prison for immortals, and that went fine, except when I retrieved the athame and he healed from the death blow, he said something that I messaged Annette about. He said, 'I honestly thought she would assign you to the cherubs. I underestimated the council's motivation to keep Santanos in power. I won't make that mistake next time.'" He pitches his voice a little higher so I know he's quoting the man, then clears his throat to resume his normal speaking voice. "Did you search the bunker when you retrieved my sword?"

Although it's a yes or no question, the assumption behind it is wrong since I didn't actually go back into the bunker. I was too busy gawking at my thunderbird. I draw the curtain and look out, exaggerating an I-don't-know shoulder shrug.

"You did retrieve my sword, right?"

I nod and then point toward Bellamy's room through the wall, mouthing his name, which just sounds like I'm popping my lips a couple of times and clicking my tongue even though I know that name doesn't have any clicks in it. Ugh. I really, *really* suck at trying to form words with my mouth. I don't know how to make the letters because I don't have any hope of making the sounds so I can't really practice on my own to get it right.

"I can't tell if you're trying to tell me something or just making random noises with your mouth to confuse me." His tone is deadpan, but the smirk teasing me makes me huff and throw a few drops of water at him before shutting the curtain again.

I hear his low chuckle, then he says something too quiet for me to hear before continuing. "Annette said she's getting Darcy to come track down the cherubs. I told her that when she finds them, we will come rescue them, but that we were having our third date tonight, and if she called us before we managed that for any reason other than rescuing the cherubs, I'd quit."

I wipe the water out of my eyes and push my hand through the curtain, giving him a thumbs up.

"I bought tickets for a dinner cruise this evening. We need to be at the dock in an hour."

I finish rinsing my body and turn off the water, opening the shower curtain without an ounce of shame.

Fox stares at me, muted by the glory of my glistening nudity. I wipe the excess water off my body, enjoying the way his eyes follow the movement of my hands, and then reach for the towel on the bar waiting for me. Fox damn near swallows his tongue when I start drying myself, proving my point that hints and peeks are more erotic than full-frontal nudity. The anticipation is so worth taking the time for.

Wrapping the towel around my waist, I step out of the shower and into Fox's space, tilting my face up for a kiss. He grabs my hips and pulls me flush against him, taking my mouth with the force of his arousal. He ravages me for several, achingly beautiful minutes, giving me everything I could ever ask for in a passionate kiss full of the promises we've made for later.

By the time we break apart, we're both hard and sweaty, and if it wasn't for the dinner cruise, I'd already be using my body to tell him, "Fuck the third date," but he went out of his way for me, and I'm not about to disregard that. We have a future full of time; we don't actually have to rush. It's more important for me to show him that I appreciate his effort than it is for me to get my dick wet. He deserves fun and romantic dates as much as I do.

Cupping his jaw and kissing the corner of his mouth, I slide past him, making sure he can feel the effect he has on me, and head to the closet to get dressed. Fox follows on my heels, pulling out a suit still wrapped in the drycleaner's plastic.

With eyes that wander over each other the entire time, we dress for our third date.

CHAPTER TWENTY-SIX

The bay at sunset is gorgeous, but not nearly as eye-catching as the man standing with me. His royal blue suit has had me sporting a semi all evening. Like I said before, the man isn't handsome, but with his black hair styled, the stubble he usually wears shaven, plus the three piece suit tailored to fit him, he looks like all my wet dreams have come true.

Plus, he carries himself with the same self-confidence that he always has, and watching him maneuver through the culture of wealth on this ship is just as sexy as watching him slice and dice with his sword. Yeah, we're on that kind of cruise. The kind where the women wear evening gowns that have precious gems sewn on instead of sequins, and the men wear half a million dollars on their wrists so they can impress each other with the size of their portfolios.

Compared to most of the people at this party, Fox and I are dressed in rags. Well, I am. My suits only cost a few thousand dollars and are definitely not bespoke. Fox's might be, but I couldn't *tell* by looking (*exaggerated wink*).

Doesn't matter, because Fox moves through this space like he owns it and the people around us are here at his leisure. When the servers come out with drinks, Fox somehow manages to make it look like they're serving him specifically. When any of the guests notice him, he returns their looks with a greeting like they should know who he is. It's incredible to watch, but more incredible is that he isn't acting any differently than he always does. Everything about him is the same as how he is when he's wearing yoga pants and carrying a sword, but in this atmosphere it makes him seem like a king.

And I hang on my king's arm and every word. I can't help it; he consumes all of my attention. And the best part is the way he's looking at me right now; he's as fixated on me as I am on him. His dark hazel eyes peer into my soul, read the words I can't speak, and tell me that I'm as important to him as he is to me.

When I saw you in the diner that first time, I decided it was love at first sight and bemoaned that I would probably never see you again. It didn't even occur to me that you'd committed a crime, I was a witness, and that if the police did their job I would be part of the reason you'd end up in prison for the rest of your life. Didn't think once about that. I was just sad that the love of my life had come and gone and I didn't even get his name.

"It was your big brown eyes that caught my attention. You didn't look scared, even though you were wide-eyed and staring. You looked sympathetic, and I couldn't figure out why some waiter in a diner would feel sorry for me," he murmurs, studying my face, looking in my eyes, then letting his gaze linger on my mouth, then back to my eyes.

It's because you ordered food and then everyone just decided you needed to die. I didn't really understand, but when I figured out that thirty to one odds weren't in their favor, I decided I was in love. Competence is sexy as hell, you know.

"I didn't expect to find you at the library. I laughed later at the look on your face when you pushed that arm and head out of your lap and gave me sass about ruining your clothes. I decided then that if I ever met you again I'd offer you a job. I haven't had a Harbinger in a decade. I went through a string of them and got fed up. They kept quitting, and they all had the same reason; they thought I didn't like them. I can't think of anyone I specifically dislike except Santanos. But that was more of an on-principle thing than a personal thing until he messed with you."

Belaphor might not have been a bad replacement for Santanos. I mean, evil is as evil does, right?

"Belaphor was right about Santanos being the council's puppet. It's better to have evil mitigated by the council than to let it run rampant, which is what Belaphor wants."

He said the council was biased against evil, which totally makes sense to me, but I honestly thought they were more neutral? Not that Omp strikes me as a neutral party.

"Actually, the fair balance of good versus evil is 90 to 10. Because evil is so visible and so much more impactful, it takes a hell of a lot less of it to make the world seem like it's falling apart. The balance was shifted by five percent in favor of evil in the 1910s and we ended up with wars and genocides for a century. We're still trying to recover that five percent. We've only managed to beat it back three percent, and that was with Santanos working with the council. I don't like him, and he is replaceable, but he's actually been an acceptable Avatar."

Why not just get rid of evil altogether?

Fox stills, searching my face again. "I think that's a serious question, so I'll give you the honest answer. We can't. Not that we won't, we simply can't. We can mitigate it, we can fight it, but the fair balance is nine to one because it takes nine people like me to stop the spread of evil done by a single person. I don't usually concentrate on Santanos' minions like I have been since we met. He caused the massacre of his own people. My usual work has me pushing back against the natural corruption of humans, like that board of directors I killed yesterday. Humans involved in such evil that the only way to regain the balance is to kill them."

I process that for a minute and land on the side you would expect. Silver linings for the win (of course I'm attracted to silver linings—bling is my thing!).

So what you're saying is, the world is 88% good. That's fucking incredible.

A crooked, happy, amused smile graces Fox's lips and he presses his forehead to mine, pulling me into an intimate hug. "That's exactly what I'm saying."

Eyes closed, savoring the closeness of my man, it strikes me suddenly that the deck has gone silent, and at the same time Fox's grip on me stiffens and he lifts his head away from mine. Before I open my eyes, I mentally warn everyone and everything in the world that if my date is interrupted and my suit gets ruined, I will rage sic my Fox on *everyone.*

Slowly I open my eyes and turn to find the silence is the result of a beautiful man stepping up onto a raised dais with a gorgeous guitar in hand. Dark mahogany skin shines under a spotlight as he sits on a stool and adjusts the microphone. He looks out at his audience for just a glimmer of a moment before he adjusts his guitar and strums a chord. His long, elegant fingers pick the notes as he begins a hauntingly beautiful melody. It feels like every person on deck is holding their breath, then his voice joins the guitar, smooth and sure, with the most beautiful tonal quality I've ever heard.

He sings in a language I couldn't even guess at, but the music and words evoke longing and love inside me. Entranced by the performer, I find myself leaning into Fox, pulled under his arm, holding onto him because I can't help but need to cling. I love him. I want him. And this music makes those emotions overflow like a cup under the torrent of a waterfall.

When the man brings the song to its end, the audience releases a collective sigh. I look up through my teary eyes to Fox, who kisses my forehead and pulls me close. "I've rarely heard a siren sing, but they tend to pull our deepest desires to the surface. Whatever you're feeling, it's an intensification of what you want the most."

I love you. I want you for the rest of our long lives. That is what I am feeling. Just love and longing for you.

Fox's breath hitches for a few moments as he reads my words, then he smiles at me, full of joy. "I feel exactly the same. I love you too."

I can't stand another moment of this life without kissing my Fox. I pull him to my lips and ravage his mouth, taking what belongs to me and giving him everything he owns as well. He tastes like my own personal dessert, a concoction of the sweetest honey and smoothest bourbon, a brulé of Fox, set on fire by the passion igniting between us.

The next song of the siren sets the atmosphere for our kiss, pressing us on, urging us to consummate our love. We don't, obviously. As soon as I realize that the siren song is pushing us toward sex, I back off from the kiss and let Fox start moving us in a slow dance designed to hide the state of our arousal. He grins at me and leans in to murmur in my ear. "If I'd known the entertainment was a siren, I would have booked us a room."

A shiver of lust runs down my spine and straight to my balls, but I manage to not cum from just his voice in my ear. Instead of releasing either his hand or his bicep so that I can talk, I give up on ever being decent in public, press my face into his neck, and enjoy the dance.

CHAPTER TWENTY-SEVEN

You know how couples in movies barely make it through their front door before they're stripping off clothing and kissing like sex is the most important thing to ever thing? That's me and Fox right now. Hands and teeth, ties flying, and shoes going who knows where. Passion. That's us.

I think someone shut the front door. Maybe. Fuck! Why are there so many buttons—never mind. My tailor's going to be pissed, but it's sexy how the buttons go pinging everywhere when Fox rips my shirt open.

And now his. Yes! Shirts off—WAIT!!!

I back up and hit a table, holding up my hands, because I'm not about to let him hurt my jewels. Not those, you perv. My diamonds. Although, yes, my balls are aching.

Fox watches me like a predator waiting to pounce as I quickly remove my jewelry.

"Godsdammit!"

The voice and the light suddenly blinking on startle me and I spin, remembering way too late that Bellamy and Darcy exist. It's Bellamy standing in the hall with his sword out and not a single stitch of clothing. Oh, and he's also pointing a gun toward us.

I'm not one to ignore the elephant in the room, so I point to his condomed dick, asking with my expression just what the hell is going on.

He growls and pulls the condom off. "It sounded like someone was breaking in!"

Darcy saunters out, also wearing nothing but a condom. What? Just… what the hell were they doing? I mean, obviously something that required both swords sheathed.

I pull my phone out of my pocket and take a picture of Darcy's dick. He absolutely turns to give me his best angle, grabbing the base of his bat and grinning at me.

"I'm waiting!" A familiar screech interrupts.

Ah. The harpy. I turn to Fox, because even I know inviting hookups into someone else's home is a bit rude.

All the ardor in Fox's expression is gone, hidden behind a blank mask. "I forgot about condoms. Can I have one?"

Darcy snickers, turning on his heels and calling over his shoulder, "I'll toss a few on your bed. Come on, Bellamy. Rowan's *waiting*."

I shake my head at Bellamy, who turns pink in the cheeks and shrugs. "Don't judge me."

We're judging you so hard. So much judgment.

Bellamy scoffs when I shove my phone in his face but has zero defense and turns tail and runs back to his bed.

I shake my head at his retreating ass.

"Kids have to make their own mistakes," Fox murmurs, pressing into my backside and working the jewelry off for me.

I'm going to ground him. No kid of mine is going to stick his dick where it's under appreciated. Did you see that thing? It deserves someone who appreciates it.

Fox chuckles in my ear, sending a shiver of desire through me. I think I might be developing an aural fixation. Hn.

"We'll discuss it in the morning. Bed now."

I'm so onboard with this plan. Leading the way, I rush to the master suite with Fox on my heels. He puts my jewels in the box he's designated for them —love that this man can keep his priorities in line—and then pounces on me, helping me out of the rest of my clothes.

More hands, tongues, teeth, skin on skin, passion and desire.

He pushes me onto the bed, following me down. My hands have a mind of their own as they explore the hard, lithe, beautiful lines of his body. He exudes strength, holding himself up as he slots our cocks together, moaning with that first slide of hot flesh.

Fuck. Yes. More.

I grab our dicks, holding them in a loose grip, grabbing his ass to encourage the gyration of his hips. He lets me lead the pace, thrusting his cock against mine until we're both panting and on the edge. Temptation to let us go off this way makes my balls draw up, but I want more than a rushed frot, so I stop him, releasing our dicks and taking a deep breath to calm myself.

Fox dips down and kisses the life out of me, moaning enough for the both of us, vibrating my lips with the erotic sounds. He straddles my hips and pulls back from the kiss, grabbing my cock and setting it against his opening. The most erotic noise I have ever heard in my life comes out of him as he presses down, enveloping me in his tight, *wet* heat. Shitshitshit. I gulp air to keep from coming, edged by the way he groans and the fact that my Fox is *wet*. We're going to save a fortune in lube!

He bottoms out, head hanging as his body twitches, adjusting to having me in him. He looks up, leaning back with his hands on my thighs, lifting his hips and letting them drop. The sight of him completely open and exposed nearly ends me, but his noises, the way he obviously loves riding my cock, makes me want to watch him fuck himself on me forever. Damn. Even in this, he's the epitome of sexy confidence, smiling like he's in absolute heaven.

Enthralled by the movement of his cock, up and down, hard and dripping, I reach out to stroke him, drawing out more of his lusty noises. I circle his length to give him friction, and he fucks up into my fist and down onto my cock in a graceful, gorgeous dance.

"Almost. Yes," he whispers, increasing the speed of his thrusts.

My balls draw up at his words, but I fight my orgasm back until I see the erotic eruption of his cum. The visual proves more than enough to push me over the edge, and I surrender to pleasure, thrusting up into him as my orgasm shoves me into black-out bliss.

When my brain comes back online, Fox and I are both breathing like we've run a marathon. He falls onto me, kissing me sweetly and nuzzling into my neck as I wrap my arms around him and just hold him like he wants me to. He clearly likes being cuddled; I knew making him my little spoon was the right decision, but this moment here proves that I am the best ever at reading people.

As my dick slips out, I wonder why Fox bothered with asking for condoms. They're right there on the pillow, easily within reach. Yeah, I didn't think about them, but I'm young. We know twenty-one-year-olds don't always make the safest decisions, though I seriously doubt STDs are an issue for Fox, and I don't have any considering I've never fucked anyone but Fox—shush you, it's not that big of a deal. I wasn't saving myself for any reason. I just didn't have the opportunity unless I wanted to whore myself out, and I never wanted that kind of job. I'd have walked to Nevada if I wanted to be a prostitute.

Anyway, point being, why bother with condoms if he wasn't going to put one on me? I honestly thought he'd be topping, so I figured he was going to use them himself, and I mean, he's several thousand years old, he really should have the ability to keep his head about him by now, amiright?

Meh. We can talk about it later. Right now, I need to get up and clean him up and tuck him in for a nap before I fuck him again. I plan to make this a *long* night for both of us.

CHAPTER 28

(OR POSSIBLY THE EPILOGUE)

The scent of coffee draws me to the kitchen. Blearily, I trudge to the coffee pot and sigh internally at the taste of toasted almond coffee on my tongue. I slide into my chair in the breakfast nook across from Bellamy, who looks about like I feel. Late nights will do that to a man, though his misery is as much too little sleep as it is bad-decision making skills.

My phone is sitting on the table along with my tie pin and pocket watch. The parts of my suit that didn't make it to the bedroom are folded on a different table. I wait until I have about half of the coffee in my cup in me before I pull my phone toward me. By that time, Fox joins us, freshly showered and looking far too chipper considering how many times I woke him up last night. That's immortals for you, fine no matter how hard you work them over.

Enjoy your night, kiddo?

Bellamy's eye twitches when he reads the message. "It was fine," he mutters.

That's good. I was wondering if your poor decisions were the reason you look like death warmed over, but if it's just how you look when you wake up, then that's fine. We'll get you on a healthy diet and exercise regimen so you can face mornings with more of a skip in your step.

CHAPTER 28

Bellamy grinds his teeth for a moment, narrowing his gaze at me. "Is that why you're such a great morning person?"

I force myself to smile past the morning grumps and meet his gaze.

Absolutely.

He grins at me. "Then I'll match my diet to yours, *Papa*. Though I think I better maintain my own exercise regimen since it's kept me alive this long."

"He has a point," Fox murmurs behind his coffee cup.

Offended that Fox is taking his side, I shoot him a glare. No, it doesn't matter that he's right; it matters that we present a united front to our kid.

Or you can take over his exercise regimen since we both want him to be better than "kept-me-alive."

Fox reads that and flicks his eyes to mine. "That's what I said."

"Is it?" Bellamy deadpans.

Fox looks at him, blank mask in place. "I always agree with your Papa."

Bellamy rolls his shoulders, trying to ease the tension in them. "I wanted to spar with you anyway."

Good. Because your life is going to be work, chores, and training with Fox for the foreseeable future. You're grounded until you learn to make better decisions. No kid of mine is going to be mooning over an asshole like Darcy.

Bellamy reads the message twice before his entire countenance turns from his normal defensive self to capitulation. "Yeah, that's fair."

My heart squeezes in my chest, making me uncomfortable with the strong emotional reaction, but I figure that's parenthood for you, too many emotions and the desire to see your kids happy especially when it's hard. I get up and walk around the table to his side and sit next to him so I can hug him, because he looks like he needs one.

Darcy saunters into the kitchen just as I pull Bellamy into my side, walking right to the coffee pot. "You have any condoms left?"

Considering we didn't use a single one?

Fox gives him a neutral look. "Nope. Your athame is on the coffee table. Shouldn't you be meeting with Annette? Make sure you walk Rowan out."

"Lord, that harpy is gone. I walked her out at midnight. I was just making sure you had a good night," he winks and wags his brows at us.

Honestly, I'd probably like him if he wasn't the person you're letting stomp all over your feelings. But since he is, I want him out as much as Fox does. Someone make it happen.

Bellamy's shoulders shake before he looks at me with a crinkly, affectionate smile. "Darcy, you better go find the cherubs; Annette isn't particularly patient when it comes to the abduction of children."

"Fuck," Darcy cusses, dumping his coffee out and abandoning his cup. "You're right. Better go find the little'uns. Thanks for the hospitality. Call me if you have need again."

In a whirlwind of motion, he grabs his athame and runs out the front door.

I lay my head on Bellamy's shoulder, thanking him for taking care of that.

Oppa totally lied about the condoms. He asked for them and forgot to use them.

Bellamy sputters into the coffee he was about to sip and shoves me off his shoulder. "I do not need to know!"

"Oh. Right," Fox hums, furrowing his brows. "We should probably use them going forward."

I exaggerate a worried expression at him.

Am I going to get sick? Is my dick going to fall off?

Fox almost smiles but shakes his head. "You're the one who told me you don't want kids." He looks at Bellamy. "We want you. You're special."

Bellamy snorts. "Thanks."

Listen, I'm not stupid. Mpreg is a thing in this world.

I scowl at Fox.

This is how people get pregnant, Fox. You needed to remind me last night that condoms will keep us from unexpected pregnancy!

"It's astronomically unlikely," he assures me. "Immortals are not very fertile no matter their species. Most couples will try for hundreds of years before they get pregnant, and the likelihood of them having more than one or two offspring in their entire existence is so low it's almost impossible."

I point a finger at him and narrow my eyes telling him he better be right.

Kids are not in my life-plan right now.

Fox gives me a solemn nod. "What about in a hundred years?"

I tip my hand side to side. Maybe.

CHAPTER 28

He captures my hand and pulls it across the table to kiss it, but of course our phones chime altogether.

We each look at the message from the depot.

Depot: *Cherubs found. Ferguson Amarro. 2225 El Dorado Dr., Roswell, NM. ASAP.*

Oh, well. I guess it's time to just up and go to New Mexico to kill a guy and rescue some cherubs. Fun.

NOTE FROM JENNIFER

Dear Reader,

I hope you enjoyed Romily and Fox as much as I did. I wrote this book just for fun but be assured there will be three books in this series. The Trouble with Trying to Get Engaged will come out summer 2022, and The Trouble with Trying to Marry a Reaper will happen late 2022 or early 2023. And maybe after that poor Bellamy will get to meet the siren of his dreams. Who knows? I just really want to write that siren; he seems incredibly interesting.

If you liked this book, please leave a review. Reviews are critical for authors like me; they help other readers find books they're going to enjoy, and they convince the mysterious and all-controlling algorithms that my books are worth putting in front of readers. Or something like that—they're mysterious… Anyway, reviews are important, and I know its nerve-wracking when you're not used to putting your opinion out there, but 20 words isn't as much as you think. In fact, it's only about two sentences. You got this (insert meme of Rosy the Riveter) and thank you.

For the love of M/M,

NOTE FROM JENNIFER

    Jennifer Cody

P.S. Read on for a peak at Bishop to Knight One.

BISHOP TO KNIGHT ONE

Deejay

"Hey Deej," my older sister greets me with a wary smile, assessing my mood as she stands next to a kid I assume she's trying to pass off as my nephew. Another guy, vaguely in his older teens, stands on the other side of the kid, holding his hand. She points to them in turn as she makes introductions. "This is Cary and Matt Blank. Boys, this is my brother Deejay Aquino, you're going to be living with him from now on."

Cary looks about four years old, bright, curious blue eyes and pale, curly, blond hair like most of our family. He doesn't have any visible bruising, which I can't say is true for every nephew that I've taken into my care. He's wearing clean clothes, but the jeans have holes in the knees and his shirt looks a little threadbare. The backpack on his shoulders is way too big for him, falling apart at the seams, and looks practically empty.

Matt stands taller than me, broader, more muscular. His tree trunk biceps bulge a little holding onto duffle bags stuffed to bursting. His clothes are just as worn out as Cary's though dirtier and with what I can tell are bloodstains spattered here and there. His shiny black hair falls in loose curls around his forehead under a worn out and faded red cap. His black eyes are set a little too far apart above a straight but overly large nose; his jaw is a little too square and wide, with a slight underbite and a five o'clock shadow that puts my ability to grow any facial hair to shame. The only indicator I have that he's a teenager and not closer to my age is the slight roundness of his cheeks as if he hasn't quite finished growing up yet.

Behind me something crashes and a scream rings through the villa-style mansion where I live.

"Come on in," I tell the boys. "Not you, Felixia. You can leave now. Don't come back for them, I won't give them to you," I remind her, though we've done this song and dance before, so recently in fact, I *know* these can't be her kids.

Felixia nods respectfully and pushes the boys into my home before waving. "See you next time, Maledict," she tells me, using the title I earned ten years ago when one of our other sisters abandoned the first son I adopted.

I shut the door on her and rush to the cries from the kitchen. "Nobody comes in here barefoot!" I yell loud enough for the whole house to hear—well, almost. It's a fucking big house.

Jasper, my six year old, stands unmoving, but crying in the middle of a debris field of broken glass. I pick him up and sit him on the counter, checking for wounds. "You ok, Jazz?"

"Sorry, Papa! I just wanted a glass of water!" he cries, hiccuping.

I ruffle his hair and kiss his nose. "Don't grow up so fast. Just ask for help until you're tall enough to reach."

"I'll get the broom, if you tell me where it is." The deep voice startles me.

I turn to Matt, who stares at the glass on the floor, looking lost and abandoned. Empathy for him wells up in me; I wish I could take away the uncertainty that I know he's going through right now. I wish that he'd been born to better parents and had an easier life, but all I can do right now is give him a soft landing after a long, hard fall. "Don't worry about it, I'll take care of it. You've only just arrived, but you are *welcome* here, and I'll give you a proper welcome after I get this cleaned up."

Matt frowns, but nods, picking up his younger brother and hugging him close. My heart aches for them, the same way it always does when one of my sisters abandons their child to me. I hate that this is the curse of the sons of Naiads, but I am glad that I can take my sister's son in—grateful that I have the clout to force my sisters to bring them to me instead of abandoning them outright like our mother did to me.

I am the youngest child of seven in my generation, and the only boy, which was fine until my sisters left my mother's care. At that point, my mother left one day and simply failed to return home again. I was angry for a long time about being abandoned by my mother and sisters, but once I matured, I learned that mine was one of the better fates of the sons of Naiads. The women of our species only care about their female offspring because only the females are true Naiads. The boys have magic, but cannot do the work of the Naiad for the waters that they tend.

Considering that there are some families out there that don't abandon their sons and instead outright kill them, I decided I could mitigate the problem in my own family. To that end, I worked hard and developed a social media platform from scratch. By the time I turned eighteen, my net worth was in the billions. I sold the company as soon as I found the first of my sister's abandoned sons, bought this villa, and proceeded to track down all of my sisters and their sons. I took their boys, and ordered my sisters to bring their sons to me with a rather vague, but effective, 'or else' threat. For ten years now my house has been a revolving door of twelve—now fourteen —of my family's unwanted males.

And it is a *joy* to have them all.

Seven of my adopted sons have already moved out of the house, moving on to the lives they want to build for themselves. I love them all, and am exceedingly proud of each of them, even the ones who are only a few years younger than me.

At dinner time, all my boys sit at the table in the kitchen for the first time with our new additions. "Everyone go around and introduce yourself," I instruct the quiet children; I know for certain that their quietude stems from how intimidating Matt is, but I also know everyone will get over it fairly quickly. He seems like a bit of a gentle giant based on the interactions with Cary I've observed over the last hour. "I'll start with the twins. These two are six months old. I brought them home from the hospital. Their names are Alex and Eren Aquino." I speak to Matt and Cary, indicating the babies that sit in highchairs on either side of me. The twins are Felixia's, which is why I know Matt and Cary are *not* her biological children. They're probably the sons of whoever her latest boyfriend is, but I haven't pried into their parentage yet. However, it doesn't matter who they belonged to before, now they're mine and I won't give them up.

"My name is Matt Blank. I'm seventeen. We're from Denver, Colorado." He speaks in a deep, rumbling voice, looking at each of us. I can't help but smile that he takes the initiative to start the introductions. I don't know him, but I think we're going to get along; he's just got the vibes of the type of person that I get along well with.

"I'm Cary Blank. I'm four." Cary speaks shyly, but follows his brother's example and looks at everyone as well. I can tell there's a lot of love between these two, and trust. Cary trusts Matt absolutely, I can see it when he looks at his brother and when they speak to each other. Matt assures him and Cary is *assured*; no doubt, no hesitation—whatever Matt tells him is *truth* for Cary.

"My name is Jasper Aquino. I'm six, and I've been with Papa since I was four too!" Jasper sits next to Cary and puts an arm around his shoulders. "I'll take care of you, because you're my new little brother!"

Sitting there with his arm around Cary, those two do look like they could be from the same tribe. Blond hair and blue eyes run in our family, but Cary, cute as he is, has some of the squareness in his face that is overly present in Matt's, whereas Jasper's is much more round and cherubic.

Cary smiles shyly at Jasper, but I can tell he isn't a naturally shy kid. He's reflecting Matt's reticence more than his own personality. "Ok."

"I'm Colt Aquino. I'm thirteen," my angriest son says suddenly, glaring at Matt. "I've been with Papa the longest, since I was three, and I'm his favorite."

I don't know why, but Colt's been simmering on the edge of rage for a few months now. The halo of his curly strawberry blond hair and his brightly innocent, round sapphire eyes belie the dark well of anger that lives inside him. He's not specifically mean to anyone, but he's quick to rage and will shut himself away from everyone when he does. I wish he would talk to me about what's going on, but since he became a teenager, things have shifted between us and I no longer hold the spot in his life as his confidant.

I click my tongue at him. "I don't play favorites," I gently chastise him.

"But yes, you were my first son." I look back at Matt to explain. "I've been taking in my nephews for ten years now. Colt is the first nephew I adopted. If I'd known about you before now, I would have brought you here already."

"It's fine," Matt assures me solemnly.

It isn't, but there is nothing I can do except give these two a stable home.

"I'm Kendall. I'm also thirteen, but I've only been here for three years," my most studious son explains, pushing his glasses up his nose.

Kendall isn't quite like the rest of my sons. First, we're barely related, having a single common ancestress four generations ago for him and five for me. Second, he's a brunet with brown eyes, and favors his paternal line rather than his matriarchal line. And third, Kendall is socially awkward in general. He doesn't pick up on social cues well in settings with unfamiliar people, though with his own family, it's barely noticeable. Rather than prevaricate, Kendall tends to speak bluntly, which doesn't always earn him friends, but it's fine because Colt is his best friend and understands him even better than I do sometimes. These aspects of his personality are symptoms of the neglect he suffered when he was very young, and he may always struggle with his social-emotional development, though years of therapy have helped immensely.

"Great, now that everyone introduced themselves, let's eat!" I clap.

"You didn't introduce yourself," Kendall reminds me, matter-of-factly.

"Oh. Right. I'm Deejay Aquino. All of these boys are my adopted sons. I'm twenty-nine years old, the ruler of the Demesne D'Aquino, and from now on, I will take care of you. If you need anything, tell me."

"We all come from different women in his family, like you two, but he adopted us all, which is why we all have the same last name," Kendall adds to Matt in his direct manner. "He will start the legal adoption process with you as well if that's what you choose, and you'll share our last name as well, but as far as everyone is concerned you are now an Aquino."

"I don't need to be adopted," Matt frowns. "I'm almost an adult already. I'll be eighteen in a month."

"Our oldest brother is two years younger than Papa and he legally adopted him. This is a family of abandoned sons, we want you to feel like you are a part of it," Kendall responds levelly.

"Speak for yourself," Colt snorts moodily.

Kendall smacks Colt upside the head. "Don't make them feel unwelcome because you have a crush on Papa."

"I do *not*!" Colt protests, rubbing the back of his head.

I chuckle at their antics. "Colt announced when he was six that he was going to make me his wife and no one's sure if he's changed his mind yet," I tease.

Colt turns bright red under his coppery blond hair and huffs. "I was a kid, of course I said something utterly ridiculous," he grumbles.

I catch just the slightest hint of a smile from Matt before he puts a bite of food into his mouth, but it makes me happy to see that he can find something to smile about.

Read more about Matt and Deejay HERE.

ABOUT THE AUTHOR

Jennifer Cody lives in Small Midwestern Town, USA, aka the sticks of Kansas. She has three kids and a Beardo she loves. Her sleep schedule is weird, so messages sent at midnight usually get answered relatively promptly. She reads all kinds of mm romance and urban fantasy, but her favorites are gay-for-you, small-town romances and over the top urban fantasy romances. Her own writing doesn't always reflect her reading preferences, but mostly it does. She writes what she wants to read and reads extensively because she's an addict. To books, obviously. And caffeine because sleep is for other people.

Join Jennifer's Facebook group, Jennifer Cody's Cocky Cuties, for all kinds of fun shenanigans, live writes, schedule updates and more!

Sign up for my newsletter on my website to get more news and occasional serial shorts.

ALSO BY JENNIFER CODY

DIVINER'S GAME TRILOGY

Bishop to Knight One

Knight to Castle Two

Queen to King Three

Forgotten Fox

(Bonus book, best read after Knight to Castle Two, because… spoilers.)

DG Short Stories

(Only available on my website. Sign up for my newsletter to get these.)

Loki Adopts a Cat

The D'Aquinos Go to War

SHATTERED PAWNS SERIES

Spinoff of Diviner's Game

Pass

Capture

Promote

Shah Mat (2022)

Houston Hub Shorts

Forgotten Fox

Mr. Monster Kok

A Knot with Santa (2022)

Genesis

MURDER SPREES AND MUTE DECREES

The Trouble with Trying to Date a Murderer

RECOVERY ROAD SERIES

Forrest's #Win

Gentry's #Doms (MMM)

Jericho's #Switch (Sign up for my newsletter to get this one)

Koki's #Life (2022)

DARK ROMANCE PEN NAME

Primal Prey Serial

By Cinnamon Sin

Watch the trigger warnings on these!

Catch Me

Episode One